"Anyone could be watching us and drawing all the wrong conclusions."

Instead of releasing her, his hands tightened. "And that would bother you, Miss Anders?" he asked, bending still nearer. "Surely you cannot care what a bunch of old biddies think of you, do you? I imagined you to be more intrepid.

"But if they are watching, let's really give them something to chew over at tea," he said as he drew her into his arms. When it came, his kiss was warm and intimate and slow, and his hands held her captive against his chest. Celia could feel his heart beating, smell the seductive scent of him. Conscious of everything about him, still she felt as if every inch of her was concentrated on their two pairs of lips, his tender yet demanding, hers afraid but still yearning. . . .

By Barbara Hazard
Published by Fawcett Books:

MONDAY'S CHILD
TUESDAY'S CHILD
WEDNESDAY'S CHILD
THURSDAY'S CHILD

THURSDAY'S CHILD

Barbara Hazard

FAWCETT CREST • NEW YORK

A Fawcett Crest Book
Published by Ballantine Books
Copyright © 1995 by BW Hazard, Ltd.

All rights reserved under International and Pan-American Copyright Conventions. Published in the United States by Ballantine Books, a division of Random House, Inc., New York, and simultaneously in Canada by Random House of Canada Limited, Toronto.

Library of Congress Catalog Card Number: 94-96483

ISBN 0-449-22317-5

Manufactured in the United States of America

First Edition: March 1995

10 9 8 7 6 5 4 3 2 1

For Lori Rood Ghidella,
who is soon to be my
"new" daughter, and who is also
THURSDAY'S CHILD

Monday's child is fair of face,
   Tuesday's child is full of grace,
Wednesday's child is full of woe,
   Thursday's child has far to go,
Friday's child is loving and giving,
   Saturday's child works hard for its living.
And the child that is born on the Sabbath day,
   Is fair and wise and good and gay.

Prologue

Miss Celia Anders had discovered quite early in life that it was difficult, if not impossible, to be romantic in an unromantic world. And that the world was unromantic, she knew full well.

Take this morning, for example. Here she was, staying in a famous posting house on the West Road, a situation that was fraught with possibilities. But had anything the least beguiling happened to her? No. She had eaten her dinner in company with her uncle, read a book for a short time, and retired to bed without incident. She had slept soundly, only waking a few minutes ago when someone dropped a heavy case outside her door.

Yawning a little, she went to the window, pulling her dressing gown on as she did so. Her room overlooked the inn yard, and she could see it was abustle with activity, even though it was still very early this gray, misty morning.

One of the five daily London to Bath coaches had just pulled in, and both the inside and outside passengers were scurrying into the inn for the hurried breakfast that was all time allowed if the coach was to keep to schedule. The tired team of four horses was being led away, the breath from their nostrils wreathing their heads, and their flanks shiny with sweat. They were strong-looking beasts, but it was obvious they were exhausted. Fresh horses were already being brought forward to replace them. The rotund coachman, clutching a large mug of ale an admiring maid had brought him, was commenting rudely on the new team. Some of the men nearby encouraged his wit by laughing heartily at everything he said.

Over to one side, a middle-aged man, neat in his country clothes, was drinking a stirrup cup before he rode away. Miss Anders saw him return it to the innkeeper with a coin in the bottom, as was the custom. There were other riders in the yard as well, and an ancient berlin whose paint was so faded it was impossible to discern its original color. Miss Anders ignored it, and a farm cart full of bulging sacks and a crate of cackling hens as well. They were not at all romantic.

Ostlers and grooms moved briskly about their business, and a dog who seemed accustomed to the dangers afoot nimbly dodged man, horse, and dung as he made a circuitous way from the stables to the back of the inn.

The lady's attention was caught by a private traveling carriage drawn up somewhat apart from the rest. The men around it wore smart livery, and the vehicle itself was as neat as a nun. Next to it was a sporting phaeton all burnished black. Hitched to it was a team of chestnuts that even the city-bred observer could tell were superior horseflesh. She wondered who owned this impressive display. No doubt some old, ugly man as rich as he was unappealing.

As she watched, a gentleman strolled into sight beneath her window, avoiding the puddles left by yesterday's rain as if by instinct.

He wore a long, caped greatcoat and a tall beaver hat, tipped rakishly over one eye. Miss Anders leaned closer, her eyes twinkling, for here was romance personified!

Although the gentleman had his back to her, she could tell by the way he held himself carelessly erect, and the restless energy of his step, that at least he was not old. And something about him made her sure he was "someone." A lord no doubt—was that a crest on the door of his carriage? she wondered, squinting a little in the uncertain light. She could not tell.

The gentleman spoke briefly to his servants, then studied the sky as if to gauge whether it would come on to rain again. At last he shrugged and waved the carriage on its way before he climbed to his seat in the phaeton and took up the reins. A small tiger took his place beside him, crossing his arms over his thin chest and sneering down at the commoners in the yard as if he were the lord, and not his master.

That man was in profile to Miss Anders now. He was not at all ugly either. She wished he would turn toward the inn so she could see what he looked like full-face, but perversely, he did not do so. Waving away the ostler who held the team, the gentleman guided the frail-looking carriage through the gates to the village street, and turned left away from London toward the west. A bend in the road moments later hid the rig from sight.

Celia Anders dropped the curtain she was holding and smiled. In a truly romantic world, the gentleman would have looked up and caught her staring at him. Perhaps he would have smiled and tipped his hat to her? Bowed, maybe? Even blown her a kiss to make her blush? Or perhaps he would have hurried back to the inn to demand her name and lie in wait for her at the foot of the stairs, struck down by Cupid in an instant.

Celia Anders snorted at her fancies as she laid out her clothes for the day. That was what would have happened in a *romantic* world, she told herself. But it would never happen in the real world, so prosaic, so conventional, so—so *everyday*. Novels lied, she reminded herself as she took a clean pair of stockings from her portmanteau and sat down to pull them on. And since that was the case, wasn't it a very good thing that she herself was not, and never had been, the least little bit romantic either?

One

"You might just as well confess what you've been up to, Dolly. You know I'll have it out of you in the end."

The Dowager Duchess of Wentworth's brown eyes widened, as if she were astonished by her companion's statement. "Up to? *Up to,* William? I haven't the least idea what you mean," she protested as she lowered her cup and saucer to the table before her.

"Doing it up too brown by half, my dear," the much younger gentleman persisted. "Inviting me, and heaven knows how many others to the castle at this time of year? What on earth are we to do with ourselves?" he asked as he waved a hand toward the graceful bay window on the other side of the drawing room.

The dowager did not bother to glance that way, for she could hear the steady rain that had been lashing the panes all afternoon. Indeed, March had been a thoroughly depressing month. The rain had fallen almost without pause, sometimes accompanied by heavy winds that set the trees to tossing their still-barren branches, sometimes teasing by promising an end to it at last by appearing as a soft gray mist. Once it had even sleeted. And from what William Welburn, fourth Viscount Drummond, could see, April promised little improvement.

"We can't fish, hunt, or ride out in this weather," he continued. "Nor will there be any pleasant

5

drives for the ladies. No, instead, we'll be cooped up together in the castle, wondering why on earth you decided on such a dreary party."

The white-haired little lady he faced drew an indignant breath and said as coldly as she could manage, "I have never given a dreary party in my life, and I'll thank you to remember it."

As he nodded in apology, she went on. "To tell the truth, my dear, I think it was because I wanted a last fling. You see, when Kendall returns from his wedding journey in May, I shall have to get me to the dower house. Not that I'm repining, mind! Far from it. Forty years' residence in the castle are quite enough for any woman to have to suffer."

As the viscount recrossed legs clad in skintight breeches and shining boots, he considered the current Duke of Wentworth. How strange it was, he thought. Dolly Farrington had had four daughters before she presented her husband with his heir, and every one of those daughters was a darling, as full of quick wit and high spirits as her mother. But the dowager's son, Kendall, was a prig; self-important, stiff, pedantic, *worthy*. This past January he had married a colorless girl from an impeccable family. The viscount was sure they would be more than content with their marriage and each other, for neither of them had a shred of imagination, nor the slightest yearning for adventure.

Reminded of matrimony, he said suspiciously, "I say, Dolly, you're not matchmaking again, are you? For if you are, I warn you, I'll have none of it."

She flashed him a look of disdain and said, "Indeed, no. I gave you up ages and ages ago. After all, you must be almost forty now, and . . ."

"I'm thirty-six, as you, my godmother, know very well."

6

"Thirty-six, then, but still a bachelor. But I daresay your cousin's son will do very well for the title, since you've taken my sex in such aversion."

He grinned at her then, a sudden, knowing smile that transformed his high-cheekboned face.

The dowager was much too old to be disconcerted. "Stop smirking at me," she commanded. "You know I mean ladies of good family! Although seriously, William, what is the difference? A female is a female, and . . ."

"You don't sentence yourself to a lifetime of boredom or endless argument with a bit o' muslin," he said promptly. "For when the time comes that she begins to nag or ceases to amuse, you give her a farewell gift and take your leave. But a wife cannot be left, more's the pity.

"Besides, you were already married before I was born, and you—and your daughters—are the only women who might have tempted me to take a chance on wedded bliss.

"But come," he added, putting down his cup and saucer to stretch a little as she clapped her hands in delight for his compliment, "tell me more of this party."

The fire they were sitting before was making him a little drowsy with the heat, although he had no intention of suggesting they move away from it. Castle Wentworth was a huge pile of gray stone, and he was sure there wasn't one of its one hundred and twelve rooms that was not afflicted with drafts and cold spots. Indeed, his hostess was wearing a warm cashmere gown with a matching stole around her shoulders, and her little feet, clad in kid boots and thick stockings she would have scorned to wear in London, rested on a footstool very close to the fire screen.

"Whom have you invited?" he prodded. "May I hope I am at least acquainted with some of them?"

"Of course you are. There will be twenty-four of us or so. I have not as yet had a response from some. But Bartholomew Whitaker and Marmaduke Ainsworth are coming, and perhaps Jaspar Howland as well."

"I know them all. Howland's only a cub, but Bart is a capital fellow; Duke Ainsworth as well."

"Then I have invited Lord and Lady Flowers. Millicent is my goddaughter . . ."

"How many godchildren do you have littering England, ma'am?"

"Only nine. Or is it ten? No matter. With the Flowerses come their twin daughters—"

"No, do not tell me, I can guess," he interrupted, looking grimly amused. "The twins are to have their first Season this spring, and they are identically, maddeningly lovely, are they not? And—dare I hope?—their names are Hyacinthe and Heliotrope? You see I remain *en garde,* ma'am, not quite trusting your resignation as regards my marital status."

"Do not flatter yourself so, it ill becomes you," she said tartly. "Besides, it is no such thing. Oh, of course they are lovely, but this will be their second Season and they have charming names."

"And they are?" he asked gently.

"Lily and Rose," she admitted. As he chortled, she went on. "I do wish you would curb this distasteful habit you have acquired of being disagreeable. If you continue, I shall be sorry I invited you."

At once he rose and came to kneel at her feet. Capturing her hand, he kissed it and said, "Fear not, darling duchess. I promise you I'll be the perfect gentleman. But only if you and I can share an occasional laugh."

She snatched her hand from his and pointed. Meekly, he returned to his seat. "Charles Danforth is coming as well," she said as if she had not been interrupted. "The poet. He is a distant relative of mine, and I did not precisely invite him. He, er, invited himself, saying he needed solitude and a bucolic atmosphere."

She shrugged. "I told him about the party, but he said in a place as huge as this, he could surely find a lonesome nook when his muse visited him."

"Hmmm," the viscount murmured, and she hurried on. "I have also asked Celia Anders and her uncle. Poor dear! But I say no more.

"Her uncle is Dudley Bell, of the Oxfordshire Bells. He is a scholar. You will hardly see him, for he will be busy with my brother Reginald. I am sure that will be best, don't you? I have found scholars add nothing to a party."

"Nor poets either. Or should I say endlessly *aspiring* poets?"

The dowager chose to ignore that last remark. "Then, of course, there is my old friend Cassandra Cousins, who is bringing her nephew's widow, Drusilla. And the Greys, Lord Manchester, Lady Powers and her son, Miss Harriet Hadley—a score or more."

There was silence for a moment, and the dowager looked at her first arrived guest with an inquiring air. He was staring into the fire now, and she admired his profile, the strong nose, his thick dark brown hair and brows, and the ridiculously long lashes he sported to match. His jaw was determined, and he had a surprisingly sensuous mouth. Not as handsome as Byron, she admitted, but my, he did have presence.

"It seems an ill-assorted group to me," he said at last. "Scholars and poets, widows and young girls, sportsmen and Darbys and Joans. But if anyone can make this party work, it will be you. You have a definite flair for such things. Besides, I wouldn't put it past you to have made up your guest list of incompatibles just to see what would happen when they were all assembled. I have often remarked your, hmm, sense of humor, ma'am."

Her silvery laughter echoed through the large room before she said, "Tell me, William, did you arrive early so you might excuse yourself if my guests were not to your liking?"

"To even suggest such a thing is to insult me, ma'am," he answered promptly. "I am sure to find a kindred spirit among them. As for the rest . . ." His shrug was eloquent as he added, "You know how conveniently deaf I can become—how vague."

The dowager watched him carefully when he left her at last, sighing a little as soon as he was out of earshot. She had not been at all truthful with him, and now she frowned. Of course she wanted William Welburn to marry—what kind of godmother would she have been if she had not? she asked herself. For a while she amused herself by reviewing the ladies she had invited to her house party, and wondering if any one of them could lure him to the altar. She did not know, for love him as she did, she had never understood him, although she suspected he had seen through her by the time he was eight. And how maddening that was.

A knock on the door roused her from her thoughts, and when the butler told her that others of her guests had arrived, she begged him to bring them to her at once.

"Certainly, Your Grace," the butler said, his voice noncommittal. He had been in the duchess's service for almost forty years, and so closely attuned were

10

they that she immediately demanded to know what was wrong.

"I was not aware that children were to be included in your party, ma'am," he said as he picked up the tea tray.

"They are not. Are you telling me someone has been so gauche as to bring one?"

He nodded. "A Mrs. Drusilla Dawkins, ma'am, who came with Lady Cassandra. A little girl, about eleven or so, I'd say."

His mistress thought for a moment before she nodded decisively. "Show them in, Bogle. Perhaps Mrs. Dawkins cannot stay and merely begs a night's lodging before she and her child travel on. If not, we shall have to see."

But her optimistic view of the situation proved to be no such thing as she discovered when Lady Cassandra and her kin joined her. Barely giving the two older ladies a chance to embrace, and to be introduced herself, Mrs. Dawkins drew her daughter forward and said, "I have such a surprise for you, Your Grace, for here is my darling daughter, Charity. I had not intended to bring her, you know, but at the last minute the daughter of the friends she was to stay with contracted an infectious cold that descended to her chest. You can see my predicament. Charity is so delicate.

"But having heard of the enormous size of the castle from my aunt-in-law, I thought that one wee bairn could hardly count. And I do assure you, Charity is the quietest child, well used to amusing herself for hours, isn't that so, dearest?"

Without waiting for an answer, she concluded. "You and your guests will rarely see her."

"Indeed?" the dowager murmured, avoiding her old friend's pleading glance where she stood a little to one side, removing her bonnet and gloves. "It is

11

to be hoped that you are correct, Mrs. Dawkins. There have been no plans made for a child, and there is no one here her age. I fear your daughter's arrival has been as unfortunate as it was unexpected."

"Never say so," Mrs. Dawkins exclaimed. "Charity will be in my maid's care and no trouble at all.

"Come, dearest, make your curtsy to our dear hostess."

The dowager bent a penetrating stare on the sturdy, almost chubby figure who bobbed an awkward curtsy. Charity Dawkins was a pale child with thin brown hair, quite unlike her mother's abundance of guinea gold curls. As she straightened, her eyes met the dowager's for a fleeting moment, and Dolly Farrington stiffened. And then she wondered why she had done so. It was not as if the child had shown insolence, indeed, her pale blue eyes, that round face, had been as devoid of expression as an empty plate. But perhaps she is only embarrassed, the dowager thought. Who would not be with such an *inching* mama?

"May I suggest you and your daughter seek my housekeeper's assistance?" she said in a voice that was more an order than a suggestion. "She will have to see to new arrangements for you, for I am sure your daughter will be more comfortable close to you. I shall have tea sent up as well. No doubt you would like to rest.

"Ah, Bogle. Kindly ask Mrs. Pope to see to rooms for the ladies Dawkins. Perhaps the maroon bedchamber, and the gold one next to it? But she will know what is best."

It seemed an age before Mrs. Dawkins stopped thanking her for her kindness and took herself away, followed by her stoic child. When the drawing room door closed behind them at last, the dowager turned an accusing eye on her dearest friend.

"I know, Dolly, I know! I did everything in my power to discourage Drusilla, but I have never known anyone so deaf to even the most blatant hint. To tell you the truth, I wonder I never noticed before this how single-minded she can be. And since she cannot imagine why any person of refinement and taste could possibly object to her adorable little girl, she is immune to entreaties."

"I don't think she is adorable," the dowager interrupted. "Indeed, there is something about her I cannot like."

"You are being fanciful, and it is most unlike you," Lady Cassandra scolded. "It is as Drusilla says. Charity is a very retiring little girl and one who was no trouble at all on the journey here. She rarely spoke and never once complained. And you know how tedious traveling can be, even for adults. But no one could ever accuse her of chattering, for most of the way she had her nose in a book. Why, sometimes I forgot she was with us for an hour on end."

Lady Cassandra paused for breath, eyeing her old friend with some trepidation. She was a gentle, quiet woman who hated strife and imposing on anyone. But when she saw the duchess's face, she had to laugh.

"Do stop staring at me in that haughty way, Dolly," she said as soon as she was able. "You know we both practiced it before the glass years ago so we could discourage encroaching mushrooms and overeager beaux. It hardly intimidates me now."

To her relief, the duchess burst into her quicksilver laugh, holding out her hand to draw her friend down on the sofa beside her. "You know me too well, Cassie. You always did. Still, you are not in my best books now. Bringing a child—for shame!

"And I tell you true. If there is any problem at all, even a tiny one, your dear Drusilla will be informed that her presence and that of her darling daughter's will no longer be tolerated at Wentworth. I am not the coward you have shown yourself to be."

Lady Cassandra sighed as she patted the duchess's hands. "I know," she said meekly. "I never did have your fortitude, Dolly, or, dare I say it, your gall? What a good thing it was you who married the duke. My gentle Henry suited me perfectly, whereas your Archibald truly intimidated me. And now they are both dead, and all we can do is mourn their passing and try to keep our memories of them fresh."

She sighed and the duchess held her tongue. She knew her friend had been truly devoted to her husband. Now was not the time to enumerate men's infuriating habits, thundering tempers, endless demands, and disgusting assumptions of superiority. She herself had had what she considered an excellent marriage, but affection had not blinded her to the duke's faults, nor had his death some ten years before erased them from her mind. But she suspected, nay, she knew, that Lady Cassandra had placed her husband on a pedestal that grew higher with every passing year.

Not for the first time, Dolly Farrington wondered that two so disparate had ever become the best of friends.

Deftly changing the subject, she began to question her guest about her numerous family, the sons, daughters, and most especially, the grandchildren.

Lady Cassandra would have been appalled to have been accused of the sin of pride, but even she could not contain the elation she felt when she considered that although Dolly had three grandchildren, she herself had eight! She had never realized that Dolly was uninterested in competition of this sort, and in reality cared very little for her grandchildren.

Time enough to dote on 'em when they were more like real people, she had told herself again and again. At the moment, they were apt to be more tiresome than anything else, and better left to the ministrations of their nursemaids, nannies, and fond parents.

Reminded of this now as Lady Cassandra told her how cunning baby Mary was, the little Dawkins girl came to her mind, and mentally she shook her head.

Just one slip, she promised herself. Just one tiny faux pas and they shall both of them be sped on their way. I shall not have my party upset, and that's final.

Two

SEVERAL MILES AWAY, an elderly gentleman stood sheltering under a large umbrella that also protected a slight, tall woman warmly dressed in a dark blue hooded cloak.

"Remind me again, my dear, exactly why we are here," he said in a mild voice. "I mean *here,* on this terrible rainy day, miles from any town or even habitation, with night coming on and the coach wheels gripped by relentless mud. I need reassurance, you see, that the end will truly justify the means."

"I am sure a stay at Castle Wentworth will more than do so, sir. And surely the little discomfort we suffer now will soon be forgotten."

Miss Celia Anders saw that her uncle was about to speak, and she hurried on. "Besides, you know how you have been looking forward to seeing Mr. Stark."

"Ah, yes, Reginald. Excellent fellow, excellent! It will be good to be able to converse in person again. Letters, while better than nothing, are a poor substitute for a face-to-face exchange of ideas."

Absently, his niece agreed, her attention more on the groom's efforts as he positioned himself at the back of the coach and waited for the coachman's bellow before he tried to push the vehicle back onto the road.

She had hoped they could reach Castle Wentworth sometime in the afternoon, for she had never been there and could hardly wait to see it. Surely it was very kind of the duchess to include her in the party, especially since they had met only once, in London the previous spring.

But now it appeared they would be lucky to arrive by nightfall, if indeed the hired coachman could be persuaded to travel on. Celia Anders shrugged. There was no sense in worrying about what might be. They would either arrive, or they would not.

She put her hands deeper into the warm muff she carried, just as the coachman cracked his whip and yelled to the groom to lay about it now! The team neighed as the lash sailed over their heads, and they leaned into the traces obediently.

It happened so quickly, Celia Anders almost missed it. One minute, the coach was tilted deep in the mud at the side of the road. The next, it stood on the road itself, the groom scrambling out of the ditch after it.

"There now, we can be on our way again, Uncle," she said as she took his arm and led him toward the carriage. "I am so glad we did not have a further delay, unloading our baggage to lighten the coach."

As she had predicted, it was full dark before they turned into the gates of Castle Wentworth and headed up the long, winding drive. Celia Anders resigned herself to further delay before she would be able to see it and the surrounding grounds. The dignified porter who admitted them to the hall bowed deeply as he told them the dowager duchess and her guests were at dinner. Perhaps they would care to retire and have their own dinners served to them in their rooms? he suggested. Thoroughly damp and chilled and well aware how disreputable they must both look after their journey, Miss Anders was quick to agree.

The porter turned them over to the housekeeper's care as the footmen began to carry in their baggage.

Following Mrs. Pope up the grand winding staircase set on one side of the hall, Celia Anders tried not to stare too obviously. What a very old place the castle was, to be sure. And yet someone had tempered its antiquity with beautiful modern hangings, lovely oil paintings, and an occasional piece of sculpture set on a shining side table. But there was also quite a draft that swirled around her ankles when they reached the landing, to remind her this was no contemporary building, and she shivered.

She kissed her uncle good-night when they reached his room, then followed Mrs. Pope down another long corridor.

"I do hope I will not lose my way here," she remarked, more than a little apprehensive.

The housekeeper turned, smiling a little. "It is a bit difficult at first, miss," she said. "But if you do not go investigating, you should be all right. I'd be happy to show you all the rooms someday soon, after you've rested up from your journey."

Celia thanked her and went before her as Mrs. Pope opened the door of a room and gestured her inside. After making sure that a good fire burned in the grate, and Celia had hot water and everything else she might need, the housekeeper curtsied herself away.

The dinner that was served to her shortly was delicious, and Celia found herself relaxing. Her room was luxurious—all velvet and brocades and polished mahogany furniture that smelled faintly of beeswax. There was a thick carpet on the floor, and the four-poster, hung with a soft green velvet material embroidered in gold thread, looked large enough to swallow her up. Celia stifled a yawn in anticipation.

There was a comfortable grouping of chairs before the fireplace, a chaise by one of the windows, even an escritoire against one wall. She went to investigate it and discovered a sheet on which was listed mealtimes at the castle, a map of the main rooms and corridors, and what amusements were to be had and when. Celia gasped a little in admiration, for here was proof of her hostess's concern for her guests.

In one of the drawers of the escritoire there was a supply of ink, quills, sand, and hot pressed paper headed "Castle Wentworth, Westbridge, Wiltshire." How very grand, Celia thought.

Still, as she took a seat by the fire again, Celia had to admit she was feeling a little nervous. Just a *little* nervous, she assured herself, for she was nine and twenty now, much too old for girlish apprehensions. It was just that she had never been to a house party before, certainly never one held in a castle. She wondered what the other guests would be like, and how she would go on. Oh, of course she knew how to behave. Her uncle had seen to that when he raised her, making sure she had an excellent governess, and all the dancing masters and other specialists to train her; it was not that she was concerned for her manners.

But she and her uncle had lived such a lonesome life! He had few friends, all of them scholars like himself. He cared nothing for the ton. Celia knew he came from an excellent background, but he had made no effort to introduce her to society. She had wondered about that a little. He never mentioned his family, and outside of a visit to his ancestral home in Kent every autumn—one which he took alone—he had no contact with them at all.

Celia's mother had been his youngest sister, who she sensed had been very dear to him, for his voice had softened the few times she had been able to get him to speak of her. She had died young, shortly after giving birth to her only child. Celia knew even less of her father. It was obvious her uncle had not cared for him; she wondered why. Since she never saw any other members of the family, she suspected her mother's marriage had somehow caused estrangement. It was something she had weaved many a dream about when she had been growing up. She did not do so now, of course.

But because of the situation, she had not been surprised when her uncle almost refused the invitation to the castle. He had written to the dowager, and for several days had gone about with a frown on his face. Her reply had made him frown even more. At last he had discussed it with Celia, saying he supposed if she should care for it, it could do no harm.

Care for it? she had thought in awe. Why, never having been anywhere, seen anyone, she could hardly wait! And so she had ordered new clothes, bought sandals, ribbons, bonnets, and shifts. Now she only hoped it would all be as wonderful as she had imagined back in London. After all, so few things lived up to one's expectations.

Miss Anders was not the first to arrive for breakfast the next morning. Miss Charity Dawkins came down very early and marched into the empty room to take a seat, her pudgy hands clasped before her on the table.

Several minutes passed before a footman backed into the room, carrying a large, heavy tray filled with covered dishes.

"Here now, and what do you think you're doing?" he asked, his sandy eyebrows raised. He put his tray down on the sideboard as he spoke, and began to light the spirit lamps.

"You're not to eat in here. Mr. Bogle told me so,"

he added. "You're to eat with your ma's maid. Hop to it, then, and make it quick!"

For a moment, the little girl only stared at him. He was not affected by that stare, for he had his back to her. At last she pushed her chair back and rose. The footman ignored her as she went out the door.

When Celia Anders entered the room half an hour later, she discovered two people were before her, although it was only a little after nine. One was a woman in her thirties whose gold curls were done up in an elaborate style. But Celia's lips curved in a little smile when she observed the gentleman who sat somewhat apart, intent on a hearty breakfast, for here was the man she had seen in the inn yard only two mornings before.

Dressed for riding, the gentleman, full face at last, impressed her no end. He was not an Adonis, but with his commanding looks, he would always attract attention. Celia saw he had armed himself with a book and wondered if he had had any chance to read it with the lady chattering away as she was doing.

Could it be that the situation was to become romantic after all? Celia wondered as she curtsied and wished them both a good morning in a steady voice.

Introductions were made all around before she selected some food at the sideboard. She took a seat not too close to either guest, nor too far away to cause remark, and began to eat with composure.

On learning that Celia made her home with her uncle in London, Mrs. Dawkins clapped her hands. "How fortunate you are," she exclaimed. "I have lived all my life in Northumberland, and I do envy you. However, after our visit here, we are to go to town for the Season."

She paused, then added with a sideways glance

at Lord Drummond, "I mean my little daughter and I are to go. I—I am a widow."

Celia expressed her condolences, but the viscount only turned a page and ate a forkful of ham. It was obvious that he felt Celia's presence excused him from joining in the conversation.

"That reminds me. I must see what Charity wants to do today. I told the duchess she would be no trouble at all, well, of course she will not. But I must be sure she is content before I begin to amuse myself. I gather the ladies generally congregate in the gold salon in the mornings to do needlework and converse. I do so hope you will be there, Miss Anders? I was beginning to despair of meeting anyone my own age here."

"I am not sure," Celia replied as she poured herself another cup of coffee. "I had thought to take a walk this morning since, for once, it is not raining. We arrived so late last night, I have yet to see the castle. I am sure it is outstanding."

"Well, yes," Mrs. Dawkins agreed, her voice indecisive. "That is if you care for the gloomy and picturesque. I prefer a more modern setting myself."

Lady Cassandra came in then, and Mrs. Dawkins jumped up to kiss her and make Celia known to her. After she had seated her aunt-in-law and brought her a plate of breakfast, she asked where the duchess might be found.

"I would speak to her of Charity," she said with a gay smile. "I understand from the butler that my darling is to take her meals apart. I do not hold with such a thing. I never have. But I could not make Bogle understand. You know these old retainers. They will act on their own initiative and then, when they are questioned, claim they had been given a direct order. I am sure the duchess never said any such thing."

22

Glancing at Lady Cassandra, Celia saw an uneasy look cross her face before it was quickly gone.

"I really would not, Drusilla," the older lady said. "If Bogle told you so, you may be sure it was by Dolly's orders. She always says exactly what she means, and I would not have you upsetting her."

"Upsetting her? Certainly not, Aunt! Such a thing was far from my mind. I only thought to speak to her and make a suggestion. If she does not feel Charity should come down for dinner, well, I suppose that will be all right, but surely she should join us for breakfast, nuncheon—"

"No," Lord Drummond said, startling everyone. So intent had they been on the conversation, they had quite forgotten him. He rose now and bowed to them. "No, Mrs. Dawkins. No child at any meal. The duchess is quite right about that. And now, if you will excuse me . . . ?"

Drusilla Dawkins looked confused as the door closed softly behind him, then she tossed her head and smiled. "I see m'lord is not fond of children," she remarked with an arch look to the others. "But when he meets my darling Charity, well, then we shall see."

Celia was happy to take her leave a short time later. It was not, like the viscount, that she did not care for children, although very few had come her way. It was just that Mrs. Dawkins's constant chatter about her little daughter's charm, intelligence, and cunning ways did get tedious after a while.

And since she had learned from Lady Cassandra that the dowager never came below stairs until after noon, she felt perfectly free to go adventuring by herself. She was not at all reluctant to avoid a morning spent in chitchat and needlework. She would meet the other lady guests soon. There was plenty of time for that.

Running lightly up the stairs to fetch her cloak, she thought briefly of her uncle, but knowing him as well as she did, she was sure he was already closeted with his old friend, Reginald Stark, and deep in some obscure philosophical discussion.

When she stepped outside at last, she discovered it was a cold, blustery day with low-hanging clouds racing across the sky, and she set off at a brisk pace to keep warm. She meant to walk down the drive until she had a distant view of the castle, and she had promised herself that unlike Lot's wife, she would not turn around until she had attained her goal. It was difficult to do, but when she reached what appeared to be a large wood and turned at last, she gasped. The castle looked so old and solid, so—my, yes—so Gothic! It might have been taken straight from one of the more brooding novels, all heavy gray stone and narrow paneled windows with thrusting turrets and ominous battlements and an air of concealing deep, dark deeds from the distant past.

The drive was lined with shubbery, and there were several paths leading from it. She was sure some were bridle paths. What a shame she had never learned to ride. But she was used to long walks, and would delight in exploring as much of the estate as she could reach that way. She had heard that more and more English people were traveling about the country, knocking on great house doors and begging the indulgence of a tour of the house and grounds. And here she was, an invited guest at Castle Wentworth. She was indeed fortunate.

As she started back to the castle, she smiled, remembering the dominating personality of Viscount Drummond. If this were a romance, how perfect he would be for the part of hero, she told herself as she reached up to hold her hood tightly against a sudden

24

gust of wind. Hopefully, there would be someone here to play his heroine. As she strolled along, Celia amused herself by wondering if he had any preferences for tall or short ladies, blondes or brunettes?

She stepped quickly to the side of the drive as a carriage approached. As it flashed by, she saw the occupants inspecting her and waving a little. More guests for the house party, no doubt.

By the end of the week, all the dowager's guests had assembled. She had had few refusals, but when she crowed about this to Lord Drummond, he reminded her that in early April, no one had very much to do, and so would be delighted to be asked anywhere.

"I declare, William, I wonder I invited you at all, you are so disagreeable," Dolly Farrington said with a toss of her head.

"I am teasing you, but you are so gullible, it is hardly worth the effort, ma'am," he retorted. The two were in the dowager's private salon, a small, cozy room that always had a blazing fire lit and was probably the only room in the entire castle without a single draft. Trust Dolly!

"I understand the doctor was here early this morning?" m'lord asked. "When I came down to breakfast, everything was at sixes and sevens, and I heard a dozen conflicting reports."

"The most unfortunate thing! One of the footmen fell down the stairs leading to the kitchens. I can't think how he came to be so clumsy. He dropped a tray of dishes and broke his leg, too, poor man."

They both turned as a knock came on the door which opened to disclose the housekeeper with a group of ladies in tow.

"I do beg your pardon, Your Grace," Mrs. Pope said, holding up her hand as if she feared the la-

25

dies might rush past her. "I was not aware the room was occupied."

"It is quite all right," the dowager said with a smile for her guests. "I gather you are giving them the grand tour? Ladies, do not let her wear you to a thread, now!"

"Yes, the castle is very large," Mrs. Dawkins volunteered.

"And so beautiful," Miss Hadley pronounced.

"Do you think so? Really?" the dowager asked, looking astounded. "Now, I myself have always thought it the ugliest place, and very full of itself, too. I do so dislike proud buildings, don't you?"

There was silence until Lord Drummond said, "Don't confuse your guests, ma'am. They haven't the vaguest idea what you are talking about. I'm not sure you do, either."

As the dowager laughed, he studied all the faces before him. Mrs. Dawkins looked suspicious, as if she thought she was being mocked, while her little daughter stared at him, her face as expressionless as always. Miss Hadley, a pale, willowy blonde in her early twenties, was blushing. The Flowers twins, identical right down to the way their black hair curled over their high foreheads, looked at each other in confusion. Only Miss Anders, he noted, seemed to be at ease. He caught her eye for a moment, and was surprised to see her nod a little, as if she understood exactly what the duchess had meant, and what he was thinking as well.

"Do run along now, my dears," the dowager said, excusing them. "As always, m'lord Drummond is right. I seldom think before I speak, and then I expect everyone to know what I'm about. It really is too bad of me."

Three

LATER THAT SAME evening, after a delicious dinner and an impromptu concert in the drawing room given by Harriet Hadley, an accomplished pianist, and Lady Powers, who played the flute and sang, Celia Anders had trouble restraining a jaw-cracking yawn. She was closeted with her uncle in one of the smaller salons, for Dudley Bell had conceived what he considered to be a brilliant idea about the positioning of the stars. Since his old friend Reginald Stark had gone off to bed, Celia was not too surprised that it fell to her lot to be his chosen audience.

As she listened to him, or pretended to if truth be told, she watched her uncle carefully. What a dear, good man he was, she thought fondly. But there was no denying he could talk the wallpaper off the walls when he got up on his particular hobbyhorse. He looked so eager now, his lined scholar's face alight. His gray eyes shone and he gestured wildly as he spoke. No wonder all the other guests had faded away when he announced his topic. Only Lord Drummond had not had to make his excuses, for he had gone early to bed with the beginning of a heavy cold.

Celia let her mind wander from the universe to the particular. It was too bad that m'lord, whom she had begun to think of as one of "our heroes," had succumbed to such a plebian ailment. It was not at all romantic of him. If he had to suffer, it should have been from a bullet wound acquired during a duel fought over the heroine, or some exotic disease that only she would know how to cure. But a cold? How common.

Of course, there were so many other gentlemen at the castle who were also hero material, the viscount could be discarded with ease if he did not come up to scratch. Neither Bartholomew Whitaker nor Mr. Marmaduke Ainsworth fit the category, although they were both of them pleasant and easy companions, as she had discovered to her delight. But Jaspar Howland, Earl Castleton, was outstanding. Tall and as handsome as sin with a brooding air, he had the Flowers twins all sighs and smiles. As for Miss Hadley—well! Drusilla Dawkins had confided that the girl was making a perfect cake of herself over him.

And then there was the dowager's young relative, Charles Danforth. As fair as the earl was dark, he had a particularly sweet smile. He was a poet, too. And poets, witness Lord Byron, could be so devastating to the fair sex. Really, Celia thought, it was all so promising.

She became aware of a sudden silence, and she smiled at her uncle. "I am sure it all sounds most exciting, dear sir," she said, rising as she spoke. "I would like to hear more when I am not so sleepy I cannot concentrate. But for now, please excuse me, and forgive me for letting my mind wander."

"It is for me to apologize," Dudley Bell said as she kissed him good-night. "I quite forgot myself. Why, it is long past midnight. Run along, do, and happy dreams."

Even as the more practical of the two, Celia did not make the mistake of suggesting he seek his bed as well. He was too excited by his new theory to do that, as she understood very well after living with him all these years. Taking a candle from the table in the hall, she made her way up the winding stair, for some reason thinking of the Dawkins child as she did so.

Surely it was unusual for one that age to be so retiring, she mused. In recalling the morning, she could not remember hearing the little girl say a word. She had only tagged along after her mother, standing quietly whenever Mrs. Pope paused to explain some furnishings or paintings.

Was it possible she had been that interested in the lecture? Celia wondered as she held her candle higher and started absently down a dark corridor to her left. Why, the Flowers twins had made no secret of their boredom, whispering together and excusing themselves as soon as they were able to do so without giving offense. Charity Dawkins certainly was a unique child.

Suddenly Celia stopped and looked around, wondering how she had reached her bedroom door without even being aware of it. With only her candle to dispel the gloom, the dark corridor yawned endlessly before her.

Perhaps I am getting to know the castle better than I had thought possible, she told herself as she opened her door and stepped inside.

She was made aware immediately that she had committed a terrible gaffe, for across the large room lit by several candles, and staring at her from the depths of a huge four-poster much like her own, was William Welburn, fourth Viscount Drummond. Even as confused as she was, Celia knew he had not invaded *her* room by mistake, for this one was done in scarlet and gold and blue, and some very masculine belongings were scattered about on chairs and tables.

The viscount was propped up on a number of pillows. In the stunned silence, his eyes narrowed and his expression changed from surprise to scorn. Celia's own eyes widened. She knew very well what he was thinking, and, shocked, her free hand crept to her throat.

"Why, good evening, Miss Anders," he said, putting down the book he had been reading to give her his complete attention. He was bare-chested, and Celia wished he would have the decency to pull the covers up over him. And then she wondered if he was completely naked under those covers, and she scolded herself mentally for such an irrelevant thought. What if he were? What difference did that make?

"I am sure you have some excellent reason for invading my room?" he went on, his voice so cold Celia could feel goose bumps come up on her arms.

"You must believe me, it is all a mistake! I am so sorry," she said, hurrying into speech. Then she had to clear her throat, it was so dry. "I was not thinking, I mean, I *was* thinking, but of something else, and I arrived here sure I had reached my own door. . . ."

"But you are in the *east* wing, are you not? That is generally where Dolly puts the maidens. Far, far from any bachelors' rooms."

"Yes, I am there, but . . ."

"This is the *north* wing."

"Well, yes, of course it must be, but . . ."

"Do forgive me that I am not more gracious and welcoming. I am not feeling very well. But stay! Can it be that you have come with your grandmother's recipe for cough syrup? Or perhaps a poultice for my chest? Hot mustard is very efficacious, or so I have been told. Or perhaps you bear a gift of hand-embroidered handkerchiefs, or you intend to offer to read to me till I drop off to sleep?"

Celia took a deep breath and stood as straight and as tall as she could, her eyes flashing her indignation. "None of those things, m'lord, not a single one. What horrid, conniving females you must have known in your lifetime."

"Well, not all of them were," he said just before he started to sneeze.

Celia was glad he had, for she really had no interest in whatever other outrageous thing he had been about to add. "God bless you," she said absently when he subsided.

"Thank you," he replied, nodding.

Celia flushed. "Again I beg your pardon for disturbing you, sir. Good night."

She had curtsied during this speech, and she turned abruptly to leave the room as soon as it was over.

"Wait!" he called in a completely different tone of voice.

Hating herself for not resisting, Celia turned back to face him. Lord Drummond's rueful little smile twisted one corner of his mouth, and when she felt her own mouth beginning to respond, she clamped it shut in a firm line.

"I have to beg your pardon as well, ma'am," he said. "I have made as grievous a mistake as you. Excuse me, if you can. It is just that, yes, some of the females I have known have been as conniving as you said. But my arrogance, assuming you were of their number, was insufferable."

Celia regarded him; broad-shouldered with strongly muscled arms and a powerful chest, lightly covered with dark hair. Her heart began to pound harder and her anger at this weakness made her voice curt as she said, "Yes, you *were* insufferable. *And* arrogant. I quite agree with you."

He seemed speechless, and she added, "But since the original fault was mine, and you have apologized so nicely, I shall give you a piece of good advice. Put on a nightshirt or your cold might well be worse by daybreak. The castle is very drafty."

"Thank you. I am sure you are right," Drummond said so meekly, Celia looked at him in suspicion.

When he sat up to throw back the covers as if to follow her advice immediately, she turned and fled. She could hear his laughter the length of the corridor as she hurried on her way. It seemed an endless time before she had turned the corner, for she could not run as fast as she would have liked, lest her candle blow out and leave her stranded in the dark. Still she could hear him, and she prayed he would not wake the entire house party with his mirth. However was she to explain it if he did?

Celia was delighted the following day when she discovered that even though the viscount had not kept to his bed, he had ridden out to Westbridge and intended to be gone all day. She was not looking forward to meeting him and looking into his amused dark eyes, possibly even having to wait for him to say something preposterous, to try and make her blush. She had watched him carefully, as she had everyone this first week of their stay, and she had come to the conclusion that he was not the type of man who would bother to hold his tongue or his temper if he did not care to.

Celia suspected he was a perfect example of all the English noblemen she had read about in that respect. They were all of them so self-centered, self-satisfied, and self-indulgent. Of course they considered the world revolved around them. Perhaps it

32

did. Everyone seemed to think so. Celia told herself she had no patience with such conceit, and would do anything she had to to avoid being alone in the viscount's company while she was at the castle.

She had no such wish as regards to Marmaduke Ainsworth and Bartholomew Whitaker, and when she came upon them that morning while out walking, she was delighted. They were standing by the lake, watching the ever-widening ripples the fish made when they jumped.

"Well met, ma'am," Mr. Ainsworth said with his pleasant smile. "Do y'fish?"

"I have never tried, being London born and bred," Celia admitted.

"Most women do not care for it," Whitaker told her. "They think fish are slimy, and they dislike the way they wiggle. And I've never met a one who would bait her own hook. Of course, they don't like removing their catch from that hook, either."

"I think you have just discouraged me from trying this particular sport," Celia said, smiling.

Bart Whitaker smiled back at her, his long face alight with amusement.

"May we join you on your walk, ma'am?" he asked. "Where do you intend to go this morning?"

"I want to investigate a path in the home wood I saw a day or so ago. Please do come, too."

"Not worried about a shower?" Duke Ainsworth asked as he fell into step on her other side.

Celia shook her head. "It is April, therefore it will rain. I refuse to be kept housebound just for that. Or do I mean castlebound?"

The three went around the lake, headed for the wood. As they walked, Celia admired the well-kept beauty of the castle grounds. Of course the rhododendrons and the azaleas were not in bloom, nor any of the flower beds, but still, it was a pleasant prospect, and promised a wealth of beauty in a month or so. She wished she might still be here to see it.

When the trio reached the path Celia had mentioned, they proceeded along it in single file. All of a sudden, Mr. Whitaker, who had taken the lead, stopped abruptly.

Celia moved forward and tried to see around his shoulder. To her surprise, he blocked her passage. "What is it?" she asked as she tugged his sleeve.

"I am not at all sure you would care for it, ma'am," he told her.

At once, Duke Ainsworth suggested they turn back.

"But this is most unfair," Celia scolded. "I would have seen it for myself if you had not come with me. And I am not a demure young miss who is easily shocked, you know."

Wordlessly, Bart Whitaker stepped aside, and Celia was hard put not to gasp. There, directly ahead in the path, was the life-size sculpted figure of a naked young man playing a flute. Seated at his feet, both arms wrapped around his legs, and with an ecstatic expression on her face, was a young girl in a similar state of undress. The figures were very lifelike.

"Why, how unusual," Celia made herself say. "But I do wonder why the duchess had it put here, don't you?"

Whitaker bowed a little as if applauding her composure. "I have heard her say how much she dislikes those people who come on procession, wanting a tour of the castle. Of course, when she is in residence, there is no hope of them getting in, but still, they do invade the grounds. I suspect she had the statue placed here in defiance and to shock them."

"Wonder if her son, Kendall, knows about it?" Ainsworth mused.

His friend snorted. "I doubt it, as I doubt it will remain when he sees it. It is well done—by Joseph Nollekens, do you think? The statue reminded me of his Venus series somewhat."

Celia had to admire Mr. Whitaker's adroitness. How easily he had turned what could have been an embarrassing episode to be snickered and blushed over into a discussion of art. She did so like him.

They had reached the main path again, and as one turned back to the castle. The morning which had begun with weak sunshine was fast deteriorating as the sky darkened to gunmetal gray, and a sharp wind forced the men to hold their hats, and Celia her skirts.

"Are you enjoying your stay at the castle, Miss Anders?" Whitaker asked next.

Celia nodded. "Very much so. I have not often been in company. My uncle, you see, does not care for it, so we stay very much to home, which I think makes an occasion such as this even more pleasurable to me."

The gentleman made some innocuous answer, and when the three parted in the front hall of the castle, and Celia excused herself to go and comb her windblown hair, Duke Ainsworth looked at his friend and said, "Know what I think, Bart? Miss Anders is a dear little woman. Wonder what her uncle was thinkin' of, to bury her away like that? She's not a girl, yet she's had no chances. It is too bad."

"Yes, it is a mystery," Bart agreed as he handed his hat and gloves to a footman. "I don't know any Anders family, but the Bells may look as high as they please for their spouses. But if I'm not mis-

35

taken, the lady doesn't seem to mind she's a spinster, and likely, at her age, to remain one."

Since Mr. Ainsworth could not agree that any woman did not lament her single state, the two took themselves off to the library for a serious discussion of the question.

But the library contained not only Lily and Rose Flowers giggling over some girlish secrets, and Mr. David Powers, who was deep in a book, but Charles Danforth striding to and fro, his fist to his brow. He was obviously so intent on pursuing his muse that the two old friends removed to the billiard room by unspoken consent. Somehow, in the course of a serious game, the feelings of Miss Anders on the subject of matrimony were forgotten.

When Celia entered the drawing room that evening, she saw Viscount Drummond facing her, talking to his hostess and Lady Powers. She was disgusted he looked so well, why, his nose wasn't the slightest bit red!

She went to the other side of the room, but only a few minutes later, as she took a glass of sherry from the tray Bogle was presenting, she heard the viscount say in an undertone, "How delightful to see you again, Miss Anders. I must tell you your advice worked wonders, for my cold is almost gone. Why, not even my mother could have shown such exquisite concern for me. I am in your debt."

"I am glad you are better, sir," came the cool reply.

"You did find your way back to your room successfully, then, ma'am?" he asked next, such a false look of concern on his face that Celia longed to hit him.

"I cannot tell you how I worried about you," he went on. "I could not help but picture you wandering endless corridors like some lost waif, knocking on doors here, there, and everywhere. I had intended to offer to escort you to your room myself, ma'am, but you left me so, er, so quickly, I was unable to do so."

Celia bit her lower lip, wondering how she was to reply, but he did not give her the chance.

"You must not be concerned about this failing you have, Miss Anders. I mean your inability to discern the correct direction. I believe many women suffer from the same lack. You have a map of the castle? I suggest you keep it by you at all times."

"Or perhaps I could just carry a small bag of bread crumbs, like in the fairy tale?" Celia suggested, entering into the spirit of the conversation. "Then, if I got lost, I would only have to follow the trail I dropped until I was safe again."

His dark eyes crinkled shut in amusement, and he nodded to her. "An excellent idea! But do employ one or the other, ma'am, for just think how embarrassing it would be for you if you were to wander off and we had to get up a search party to find you before you starved to death."

"A search party, William?" the dowager asked from behind him. "Whatever are you talking about?"

"I was just warning Miss Anders how dangerous it could be if she wandered off alone here. The castle is so huge."

Dolly Farrington put her head to one side in thought. As the other two watched, a look of anticipation and delight appeared on her face, and the viscount raised his hand. "No," he said firmly. "Whatever devilish scheme has just come to mind, no, ma'am. Absolutely, no."

"Spoilsport," the dowager scolded. "Besides, it is no such thing. It will be delightful fun. And I have no intention of allowing my party to dwindle into dullness. I have a number of things in mind—remind me to tell everyone about them after dinner."

Celia had relaxed as soon as the dowager appeared, but when she moved away in response to Lady Cassandra's beckoning hand, she was on guard again.

"I understand you are a great walker, Miss Anders," Drummond said next. "You do not ride?"

As she shook her head, glad to be able to deny that talent, he added, "A pity. You can see so much more of the grounds and the countryside on horseback. However, all is not lost. You must allow me to tool you about in my phaeton the next pleasant day. There are several outstanding views you should on no account miss, and a delightful medieval ruin only a few miles from here that most ladies find entrancing."

"I do not care for ruins," Celia was quick to say.

"Somehow I was sure you would not," he said at his blandest. "I hate 'em myself. How grand it is that we find ourselves in such accord.

"Ah, I see Bogle is about to announce dinner. I shall do myself the honor of seeking you out later, Miss Anders. You are such a delightful conversationalist."

Celia told herself she would not allow the disturbing viscount to upset her or ruin her excellent dinner. Unfortunately, this evening she was seated with Charles Danforth on one side, and her uncle's crony, Reginald Stark, on the other.

Mr. Stark asked her if she was enjoying herself, told her how fortunate she was to be related to her brilliant uncle, and recommended she try the mushroom sauce. This seemed to exhaust his conversational tidbits for the evening, and he retreated into deep thought.

Mr. Danforth, on the other hand, was voluble to an extreme. He confided to Miss Anders that he had achieved what he considered a major breakthrough that very afternoon. What did she think about him changing his specialty from poetry to prose? Not allowing her to answer, he enumerated all the benefits to be derived from such a move, and without intending to, inadvertently revealed why he thought to do so at all.

"That damn—I do beg your pardon, ma'am!—that Byron fellow has turned everyone's heads. I can't see what's so special about him myself. But since he has appeared on the scene with his *Childe Harold's Pilgrimage,* there is no getting anyone to read one's own work at all."

Celia said she could understand his disappointment very well, but when he asked if she had read any of Byron's works, was forced to confess she had. "And very touching I found some of it, too, although of course I did not like *everything,*" she added when she saw Mr. Danforth's face fall.

"I am sure you must agree the man's a charlatan," Danforth went on. "It is too bad he is noble. A commoner could be put in his place more easily. But Byron, now, well, he's spoken of in Parliament, and not only Caroline Lamb but Lady Melbourne have taken him up. What's to be done?" he finished, throwing out his hands as a footman removed his almost-untouched plate.

"Perhaps you would enjoy writing a novel, sir," Celia suggested.

He blanched, staring at her as if she had suddenly turned into some strange, otherworldly creature. "Surely you jest," he said at his most haughty. "*I* write a novel? Besides, writing is not enjoyment. It is the most exquisite agony! The hours I have spent trying to decide between two words—but, of course, such things are beyond your understanding. I must not be too harsh."

On his other side, Lady Cassandra questioned him just then, and he turned away. He made no effort to engage Celia in conversation again. She told herself it was very bad of her to be so relieved. Instead, she ate her dinner and watched and listened to everyone else at the table, storing up absurdities to examine and enjoy later.

Four

AFTER DINNER, WHEN the ladies left the gentlemen to their port and retired to the drawing room, Celia went to study a painting of the duchess that was hung over the mantel. It had been done when the lady was much younger, but even so, you were sure to recognize the Dowager Duchess of Wentworth in the smiling young beauty of the portrait.

"I see you are admiring the Gainsborough," the dowager said as she came to stand beside her.

Celia thought that was an odd way to put it, and she smiled. "No, I was admiring Gainsborough's subject. What a beautiful girl you were."

Dolly Farrington patted her hand. "Well, I was not an antidote by any means, but still Thomas did idealize me. He was just the tiniest bit in love with me, so the dear man must be excused."

She paused for a moment, as if to organize her thinking before she added, "But I imagine an artist must always fall in love with his subject, don't you? He spends so much time staring at her, it is only natural he begins to make her the perfection he sees in his mind's eye. And I know for a fact *realistic* painters never truly succeed. One wants to be idealized, doesn't one?

"Of course I flirted madly with him, so I am much to blame. I must tell you, Miss Anders, I was an incorrigible flirt. And why did I say 'was'?"

Celia gurgled with laughter. How much she liked Dolly Farrington!

"Come and sit with me, dear. We have had so little time together," the dowager said as she led Celia to a sofa. "You are comfortable with the other guests?"

Celia assured her she was, and Dolly Farrington nodded. "I am so glad to hear it. William—Viscount Drummond, you know—told me I was tempting fate to assemble such a disparate group, but it has all worked out very well."

Celia wondered why that man's name had to come up at every turn. She hoped her face expressed only mild interest.

"Now, my dear, I have something I would like to talk to all the ladies about, for the gentlemen will be joining us soon, and we must make some decisions before then. If we wait, nothing will be done, and that would be too bad."

She rose and clapped her hands, calling for attention, and, intrigued, the women in the room drew closer.

The dowager began by telling them how happy she was they had all come to the castle, and how she hoped to make their stay enjoyable. She then told them her gardener had predicted the rain would continue for days. Several faces fell, notably those of Miss Hadley, who had been dreaming of a cross-country ride with Earl Castleton quite, quite alone, and the twins, who were planning encounters of their own with the party's handsomest young man.

"But we must not despair," Dolly Farrington went on, shaking an admonitory finger at them. "No, indeed, for there are so many things we can do to amuse ourselves right here in the castle. First, may I suggest we begin practicing a play? I am sure my young relative, Charles Danforth, can be helpful there, choosing something that will not be too difficult to learn. Then, just before your departure in two weeks' time, we can invite the local gentry, even have the servants in to swell the audience for the performance."

Several of the ladies nodded, but others, notably the older ones, pulled down their mouths and whispered a little, for not a one of them considered Dolly Farrington a proper judge of what was and what was not suitable for the young, even in amateur theatricals.

"Tonight we will have an evening of children's games. I have already sent a footman to the nursery to find them. And there are so many others! Remember Hunt the Slipper? What fun that was! And Going to Jerusalem! We'll have prizes, too!"

Drusilla Dawkins clapped her hands. "How delightful, ma'am," she enthused. "I shall send for Charity at once! It is not a bit too late for her, and she will enjoy it so. . . ."

"No," the dowager said baldly. "Perhaps she would enjoy it, but I can assure you no one else would. I have told you before, Mrs. Dawkins, your daughter is not welcome at adult revels."

The eager mother subsided, but her color was high. Celia felt a little sorry for her. She was such a sensible woman except where her daughter was concerned.

"Of course, we must have dancing," the dowager continued. "There are some excellent musicians in Westbridge. I shall engage them tomorrow. And what say you to an evening of charades?"

The ladies all nodded a smiling agreement. Charades were unexceptional.

"And I have had the most delicious idea. Gambling! Oh, not, of course, for money. Perhaps just for tokens or toothpicks or something. We can play *rouge et noir,* faro, hazard, deep bassett—I know the gentlemen will be glad to assist me in setting up a gambling hell right here in Castle Wentworth, as well as telling me how we should go on."

Mrs. Grey looked shocked, and Lady Flowers shook her head decisively. "How can you even suggest such a thing, Dolly?" she asked, in her distress quite forgetting the title she always used. "It is most unsuitable! And with young girls here, too. Albert will never permit it."

The dowager appeared to consider this carefully, while the twins exchanged anguished glances at being singled out. "But, Millicent, don't you think it would be a good learning experience for them?" she asked at last. "For to my knowledge, no one ever wins in gambling hells except the bank. One is always hearing of some young idiot who has lost his entire fortune in one, and has to be restrained from blowing out his brains.

"Perhaps losing a large amount of counterfeit money might just discourage them from gambling for life?"

The older ladies did not appear at all convinced by this reasoned argument, and their hostess shrugged.

"Oh, very well, we shall forget that part of the program. But I am sure there can be no objection to a game of hide-and-seek, now, can there?"

Barely pausing to see if there was an opinion for or against, she hurried on. "Viscount Drummond said something before dinner that put the idea in my mind. Since the castle is so very large, I think we should confine the game to only the oldest part. Some dreary, rainy afternoon, shall we say? That way we will not have to contend with candles."

The older ladies, relieved she had given up the

gambling scheme so easily, were quick to nod their approval, and the younger ones began to scheme anew about how to get Jaspar Howland, William Welburn, or Charles Danforth alone in some distant room for a rendezvous.

When the gentlemen came in, they were surprised to hear the hum of conversation, the bright smiles and laughter. Generally, the ladies seemed subdued when left to their own devices. When apprised of the reason for such vivacity, they could do nothing but agree. Somehow, in the short hour they had been closeted with their port, it had all been decided, and there was nothing they could do but go along. Dolly's work, of course, Drummond told himself as the footman brought in the spillikins and the game of fish, and began to lay out the counters.

To everyone's surprise, the retreat to childhood made for an enjoyable evening, and if some of the elderly guests missed their usual game of whist, they were wise enough not to say so.

Charles Danforth turned out to be a demon at spillikins, but Rose Flowers won handily at Going to Jerusalem. Bartholomew Whitaker excelled so at cross-purposes that he was excluded from the game of crambo. Viscount Drummond won that with ease, for there was no one except him who could find a good rhyme for incredulous.

In all the excitement, there was no chance of any private conversation. Celia told herself she was relieved, for she had not been looking forward to the viscount seeking her out to tease her again. Even, she wondered why he would bother to do such a thing. The other, younger ladies in the party were so much prettier, so much more accomplished. It was a puzzle.

William Welburn was not at all sure why he did

it himself. Perhaps because he was tired of pretty young things, all airs and graces and blushes and wiles? Perhaps because he sensed Miss Anders was not completely at ease here, and wondered what the mystery surrounding her might be? Perhaps because he had seen the tiny smile she was so quick to discourage when one of the other guests did or said something absurd?

The next morning, at everyone's breakfast place, or carried up to them on their trays, was a request to assemble in the great hall at noontime to discuss the amateur theatricals to be given. The play was to be chosen then, and parts assigned. There were also people needed to oversee the set making—to be done by the estate carpenters—and costume design—to be carried out by the ladies' already overworked abigails—and such other activities as would be needed to produce a play worthy of Drury Lane.

Celia read her copy of the request with some amusement. She had no idea if she could act, and had no intention of finding out. Instead, she would volunteer for costumes, or prompting, or something that she could do behind the scenes. Drusilla Dawkins, who was beside her at the table and still feeling depressed because Charity had been rebuffed yet again, sniffed in derision.

"Of course it will be just like Her Grace to veto any play that has a *child* in it," she said, tossing her head.

"I most certainly hope so, ma'am," Mr. Grey said, lowering yesterday's London journal to glare at her over his spectacles.

Mrs. Dawkins ruffled up, and Mrs. Grey sprang into the breech. "So unsuitable for the young, the theater," she hastened to say. "One would hate to have a child's mind bent in that direction, ain't that so, dear ma'am? And from what you have told me, your daughter—little Cherry, was it not?—is so advanced, who knows what might not result if she were to be enticed to a life on the boards."

"Her name is Charity," Mrs. Dawkins said between clenched teeth.

"Of course it is," Mrs. Grey said absently. "Please pass the jam, Miss Anders, if you would be so kind."

But when Drusilla Dawkins went away, and Mr. Grey took himself off to the stables, his wife remained at the table, toying with a piece of cold toast.

Celia wondered why. She had had several conversations with the lady, and had stigmatized her as a maggoty, tiresome woman who spent most of her time trying to put her husband's insults in a more favorable light. Celia had spent a dinner beside Mr. Grey. She sincerely hoped she would not have to repeat the experience.

"My dear," Mrs. Grey said now, leaning forward, her faded blue eyes wide as she lowered her voice. "I have heard the most shocking thing! Can it be it has come to your ears as well?"

"I really couldn't say, ma'am," Celia said, hoping someone else would come in and interrupt this unwelcome tête-à-tête. She had no urge to discuss whatever hot tidbit of gossip the woman had dredged up, but she could see there was no escape for her.

"It concerns Lady Powers," Mrs. Grey explained. "Of course, everyone knows she and her husband have been at daggers drawn for years, and have not lived together since the birth of their son, David."

Celia sipped her coffee calmly. She had not known.

"But I have learned that besides estrangement, Lady Powers is currently conducting what one can only call an affair. And at her age, too. Hmmph!"

Celia inspected her fellow guest. Was it her imagination, or was Mrs. Grey's indignation at this slip from grace less a disgust of the lady's morals than envy she was still able to attract a lover? The two were much the same age, after all.

She realized Mrs. Grey was waiting for her to comment, and she said, "I did not know. Indeed, I am not at all familiar with society, living apart from it as I do."

"How ghastly for you," Mrs. Grey crooned, momentarily diverted, before she went on all in a rush. "But that is not all. Lady Powers's lover, as I have it from an impeccable source, is *here*. Right *here* at the dowager's house party! And there have been several trips through the dark halls in the dead of night. Isn't that disgusting?"

"But it might not be so. And if that were to be the case, wouldn't it be better not to repeat a rumor, ma'am?" Celia said, rising and smiling a little to take the sting from her words.

"I assure you there is no chance my information is erroneous," Mrs. Grey said, looking militant. "I feel it is my unpleasant duty to inform Her Grace what is occurring under her stately roof."

Celia had a sudden vision of Dolly Farrington's astonished face, the silvery laughter she was sure to succumb to, and she had to contain a chuckle herself.

Mrs. Grey did not appear to notice. "You see, Miss Anders," she said earnestly, "it is the duty of the women of the world to uphold moral standards. Such a sacred trust cannot be left to *men*. Certainly not! If it were, the world would go to hell in a handbasket almost immediately. No, it is women who must stand firm in the vanguard, shoulder to shoulder, banners held high . . ."

Celia could only breathe a sigh of relief as the door opened and Mr. David Powers came in. He was a short man in his early thirties, already going bald, a widower with three small children. Celia had admired his quiet good sense, his pleasant face, and conversation many times before. She wondered if he knew his mother was being gossiped about.

"You must excuse me, ma'am," she said, curtsying to them both. "Sir? Give you good morning."

Powers grinned at her from the sideboard, where he was selecting a kipper. Behind him, Mrs. Grey, her color high, was gathering her belongings, preparatory to quitting the room. Celia fled.

In the library, she found Bartholomew Whitaker and his cousin Jaspar, Earl Castleton. It was raining again, a hard rain that beat against the library windows. There was small chance she would be able to take a walk today, Celia thought, and she sighed as she went to select a book.

"Shall you be in the hall at noon, Miss Anders?" Whitaker asked from the depths of a large chair. "I gather that was a royal decree we all received."

"Oh, yes, I shall be there," Celia told him. "I have no talent for acting, but perhaps I could do something else."

"Her Grace will probably set you to copying out parts," Earl Castleton said as he folded his journal and prepared to join the conversation.

But the Flowers twins entered the room, and Celia saw Bart Whitaker shake his head almost in warning to his younger cousin.

"Oh, m'lord!" both girls said in unison as they came to curtsy. Lazily, the earl rose and bowed.

"Just the man we wanted . . ."

"To see. Are you going to . . ."

"Be in the play?" they asked, one after the other.

"I do hope so, for it . . ."

"Won't be anywhere near as exciting if you aren't."

Celia thought the twins looked enchanting this morning. Dressed identically in pink sprigged muslin with only matching stoles to ward off the drafts, and with the color coming and going in their cheeks, they were a sight to gladden any gentleman's heart. Then she wondered if the earl ever tired of being pursued, ever wished to live the life of a hermit to escape it, and her lips curved ever so slightly. She could not imagine that handsome young man as a hermit, no, not by any stretch of the imagination. Besides, it would not be just. He was so very much the "hero."

As the twins continued their animated conversation, Bartholomew Whitaker came closer and murmured, "Dare I ask what you are thinking, Miss Anders? There is that about your expression that intrigues me."

Celia looked up at him, laughter written clear in her hazel eyes. "Perhaps I might tell you if it did not concern your cousin, sir."

"Jaspar? Well, he would probably enjoy the joke as well. He's come a long way these past few years. A *very* long way.

"There was a time he would have been rude to those girls in so obvious a way, it would have sent them crying for their mama. But he has come to see there is no harm in females like that. They are only young and foolish. And since he sees his face in various mirrors every day, he must excuse them their idiotic devotion."

"Oh, dear sir, surely you don't mean that . . ."

"We should be *actresses*!" Rose-Lily exclaimed, their voices rising in delicious horror.

"What a pity no one has ever told them why they will never get a husband between them," Whitaker said in Celia's ear.

"But of course they will," she replied, much shocked. "They are so lovely."

"True, but more than beauty is required, at least for most men. There must be some intelligence, some depth of character, some caring concern for others. And tell me, have you ever heard one of them complete a sentence? Of course not. They have been so much in each other's pocket that they have become accustomed to speak as one. Since bigamy is a crime in England, what's a man to do? He cannot propose to both, and yet both would probably insist on being present."

Celia had begun to chuckle long before he finished, and now she said, "Perhaps their mama might look about for identical twins of the opposite sex for them?" she suggested.

Whitaker gave a shout of laughter that caused his cousin and the twins to look up in inquiry, and William Welburn, who was entering the library, to pause for a moment in astonishment.

Celia saw him from the corner of her eye and turned back to the shelves, determined to select a book and make herself scarce. She had been able to avoid him last night; she did not think she would be able to do so today. And from the determined way he was coming toward her, she guessed that was very much on his mind.

He greeted her and Bartholomew Whitaker easily, mentioned the inclement weather, and the dowager's scheme to present a play.

"I think Miss Anders ought to try out for one of

51

the parts," Whitaker said. "However, I suspect she will not."

"You do not care for acting, ma'am?" the viscount asked, his dark eyes keen.

"I have no idea," Celia said honestly, thinking it most unfair that a man should have been blessed with that dark sweep of eyelash. "I know only I wouldn't care to be the focus of every eye. Much better to let others have the glory."

Her eyes twinkled again, and as she gave that little chuckle that was so endearing, Whitaker said, "Come, come, ma'am! What are you thinking now? It is not at all kind of you to keep the best jokes to yourself, you know."

"Why, it occurred to me that it would be easier if the Flowers twins played the heroine."

"But there can only be one heroine," the viscount pointed out.

She nodded. "But they are so alike, who would know when Lily retired behind the curtain and Rose came on to take her place? You see how ideal; they would each have to learn only half the role."

Both gentlemen applauded her wit, and Celia dropped them a mock curtsy before she turned and took down the first book that came to hand. "Excuse me, sirs," she said. "I have been longing to read this."

As the door of the library closed behind her, Bartholomew Whitaker laughed a little. When Drummond looked at him, he said, "Now, I wonder why Miss Anders would be at all interested in one of the late duke's stud books? From the year 1789, too."

The viscount saw where he was pointing. There was a book labeled 1788, a space, and then one for 1790. It did seem strange, unless you knew, as he did, that the lady had only been trying to escape. He would make her pay for that, he promised himself as he cocked a brow at Bart Whitaker and went to find one of the London journals to read.

Whitaker watched him intently for a moment, wondering what he was up to. Miss Anders, for all her pleasant features, her slim, curved height, and the heavy chestnut hair she wore in the classic chignon that was so unfashionable, was not at all Drummond's type. Not even her speaking hazel eyes could redeem her.

Why on earth was he interested?

Five

THE VISCOUNT WONDERED about that himself as he settled down in a comfortable chair with the paper. After all, although Miss Anders was passing attractive, she was no beauty. Then her unusual eyes, all green and brown with the golden specks in them, came to mind, and that engaging chuckle she gave when she was trying very hard not to laugh out loud, and he smiled.

He knew she was well past the customary age for marrying—a woman rather than a girl. He wondered why she had never wed. Perhaps she was a shade too tall, a bit too thin for most tastes, but still ...

What family had the dowager said she came from? Ah, yes, the Oxfordshire Bells on her mother's side. He was not familiar with anyone named Anders, but with the Bells behind her, her father's family would not matter. Surely her uncle had been most remiss not to see to her marriage long ago. And come to think of it, that was unusual, too. Why had Miss Anders been raised by an old bachelor? Why not one of her aunts, or a female cousin, or someone like that? Perhaps he would have the chance to ask her about it someday.

In the meantime, he would continue to seek her out. It would amuse him, and perhaps intrigue her, even for this brief time they would be together. And she did have such a unique way of hiding that little smile she could not always keep under firm control. He had found himself looking for it whenever someone in this ridiculous house party of Dolly's spoke up or acted out.

Only Reginald Stark and Dudley Bell were absent at noon when the dowager swept down to the great hall. Everyone else was present, milling about and talking of other plays they'd seen or performed in. Charles Danforth was very full of himself, for he had spent the morning with his hostess choosing a play. And even though she had vetoed most of his suggestions as being too heavy or too difficult to learn or stage, and once even, to his disgust, too dull, they had finally settled on a three-act play set in the past century that the dowager happened to have to hand. It was almost a farce as well as a bit of a mystery, which she claimed was the best thing for this group. It also had a number of parts, some of them brief with only a few lines, another important factor.

Only two male actors had much to memorize, and only one actress. Dolly assured him the play would be perfect, and when she saw he was still pouting, begged him to consider the role of hero, for, being a poet, she said, he was the only one who could do justice to it.

An hour later, the play was cast. Danforth would be the hero, and Bartholomew Whitaker his friend. William Welburn found himself playing the villain, and his godmother pretended she did not see his sardonic look. Miss Hadley was chosen as the heroine since the twins could only blush and giggle when given lines to read. Somehow or other they ended up sharing the role of murder victim.

Earl Castleton refused to act; instead, he became the director of the play. Everyone was given something to do, and when it was pointed out to the dowager duchess that there would be hardly any audience, she opened her eyes wide and declared she was sure *she* would enjoy it, and her neighbors and all the servants, too.

Celia could not be persuaded to read, but she volunteered to copy parts and help wherever she was needed. Lady Powers agreed to copy, too.

Her smile for Celia was bright and warm, and Celia was reminded of what Mrs. Grey had revealed that morning. Her eyes sought Lord Manchester, where he lounged against the mantel. He was a tall man in his late fifties, with a distinctive profile and a firm jaw. His white hair was swept back from a noble brow, and his dark eyes were still keen. As she watched, Celia saw him nod a little to the lady beside her and smile, and she wondered if perhaps Mrs. Grey had been right after all.

"We must get to work somewhere at once, but where, Miss Anders?" Lady Powers said as she gathered up the sheets of the play. "The library is too much occupied. Perhaps there is a small salon somewhat apart that we could use? I'll just speak to Bogle and we can begin."

"I guess it is just as well it is raining," Celia told her a little later as the two settled down with a quantity of paper, quills, and a fat inkpot between them. "At least we will not be tempted to run away for a drive or a walk, and shirk our duty."

The two worked diligently for over an hour before Lady Powers put down her quill and massaged her fingers. When Celia looked up, Lady Powers said, "I have a touch of rheumatism, and writing bothers me a little. No, do not be concerned. It is quite all right, and the exercise is good for it. Still, may I suggest a short respite for a cup of tea?

"It is the least we should expect, slaving away here by ourselves," she said as she came to take her seat again after giving orders to a footman. She smiled and added, "I have been meaning to ask you how it is we have never met before this, Miss Anders. I know most of the ton, yet you are a stranger to me. And surely I have heard your home is in London?"

Celia explained her situation.

The older lady looked as if she were staring at something a great distance away. "Hmmm," she said at last. "Now, why am I so sure there is something I know . . . Ah, well, it will come to me.

"You must be sure to call on me this Season, my dear. David and I reside on Brook Street, and we would be so pleased."

Celia was quick to agree. No matter what Lady Powers was—or was not—doing with Lord Manchester, she was a pleasant woman, and a kind one. No one else had suggested she call on them in town. But Celia had come to see that people in society were even more selfish than anyone else, and the women were as guilty of this unattractive trait as the men. Only when they were happy did they deign to consider the rest of humanity, however casually.

Her musings were interrupted by the footman who came in bearing a large tray. Behind him, Celia spotted little Charity Dawkins going by in the hall. The child seemed to pause for a moment, staring in at them, and Celia wondered if she was looking for her mother. Before she could inquire, however, the child had disappeared.

"How lonesome Charity Dawkins must be," she remarked to Lady Powers as she poured out. "Surely it must be difficult for such a little girl, with no one here to talk to or play with."

"I wonder Mrs. Dawkins brought her, indeed I do," Lady Powers replied. "Most unsuitable. And although she dotes so on the child, I have to wonder why. For even taking into account a mother's blindness, the child is so unattractive, so silent, so—so strange. I was remarking it to David only a few days ago."

"I could not say. I don't know how children should behave, never having had anything to do with them," Celia said truthfully.

The rest of their respite was devoted to a monologue given by Lady Powers describing her delightful grandchildren, and how sad it had been when her son David's wife had died. When Lady Powers squeezed her hand in parting, Celia told herself she was only imagining the woman was looking for a replacement. Still, she was delighted she had made a new friend.

The rain had stopped, and now, in the late afternoon, the sun had slipped below the clouds. Celia threw on her navy cloak and left the castle, walking briskly and breathing deeply of the damp air in her delight to be outdoors. She had at least an hour before she need dress for dinner, and she intended to make the most of it.

She set off down a bridle path for the first time, sure she would not meet a horseman this late in the day.

At first the path wound through a section of woods. Celia grinned at a squirrel who waited until he was safe on a high branch before he began scolding her. When she came to an open field, she paused for a moment to watch a pair of hawks drifting across the sky in ever-widening circles. They looked so innocent, until you remembered they were seeking prey.

Back in the woods again, she came to a bridge that spanned a rain-swollen stream. For a while she watched the stream's mad dash over the rocks below her. It was very noisy. At least that is what she told herself later to excuse the fact she had not heard the horse as it cantered toward her.

"Miss Anders, well met," Viscount Drummond said in his pleasant baritone. Celia whirled, gripping the railing of the bridge with hands suddenly gone white at the knuckles.

He dismounted and came toward her, leading his horse. "But, ma'am, you're as pale as a winding sheet. Did I startle you so badly?"

She took a couple of deep breaths before she nodded. "I thought myself completely alone, and the noise the stream makes hid the sounds of your approach."

He was frowning now. "Generally, it is not a good idea to walk on bridle paths. You could have been injured, for some mounts are not only bad-tempered, but easily spooked."

Being scolded made Celia feel as if she were no more than two. "I am sure you are right, sir. But it is so late in the day, I did not expect to meet anyone."

As she spoke, she wished he would not stand so close to her, but something told her that if she retreated even a tiny step, he would know why, and taunt her with it, and she concentrated on holding her ground.

"Speaking of late, it is all of that," he said. Pointing his crop at the sky they could see beyond the bare branches above them. "Best we start back to the castle, lest we get caught out here after dark."

"Of course. Please ride on, sir. I can find my own way."

He pretended astonishment. "What, leave you here alone, ma'am? I will not. Who knows what dangers might not come to you if I did such a thing? No, I'll walk with you and lead the horse."

Celia could think of nothing to say in reply, but when she tried to edge past his mount, the horse stretched out its neck and nuzzled her shoulder as if to keep her prisoner. Viscount Drummond chuckled.

As they started off, Celia wished she were not so aware of the man. It was as if all her senses were on the stretch against her will. She could feel not only the strong masculinity of him as he kept pace so close beside her, but smell the warmth of his skin, and the lotion he used on it. Mixed in with that was the earthy aroma of the decaying damp leaves in the path, stirred by their feet. Celia knew she could touch him without even having to reach, and then she wondered why she had thought of doing such a thing. Such images were dangerous, better left unexplored.

"What are you thinking about?" he asked as he glanced down at her.

"My thoughts are my own, sir," she said, glad it was so.

"Of course they are, but that telling blush you sport informs me just as clearly as if you had done so yourself that you are thinking about me. Well, why not? I have often thought about you since you invaded my room so late at night, and then ran away before any good could come of the adventure.

"Tell me, ma'am, why did you turn fainthearted?"

"I told you it was just a mistake! I . . ."

"So you did. But have you ever considered how the mind plays tricks on us? That sometimes when we are not consciously thinking of something we want, it leads us in paths of its own devising? Consider dreams, ma'am. Some of them make a great deal of sense, yet our minds conjure them up without our aid.

"Perhaps you *were* thinking of me that night, and

all unbeknownst to you, your mind guided your footsteps until you found me."

"What an odiously conceited thing to say," Celia exclaimed, not only shocked but embarrassed. What would he say next? Do? And they were still so far from the castle!

He stopped and grasped her arm to turn her toward him. "No, it was not conceited, it was just a fact. And if you were not such a timid little mouse, you would admit it. I have done so. For what is wrong with wanting to be with someone you are attracted to?"

"And you would have me believe that you are attracted to *me?*" Celia asked, astounded. "Oh, no, m'lord! For you never paid me the slightest bit of attention until I blundered into your room all in error. Now you seem to be pursuing me. If you do so out of politeness because you mistook the matter, or to pass the time while you are here, that is bad enough. But if you do so because you see no reason not to take advantage of something you think was offered for free, that is worse. Believe me, I did not come to your room either deliberately or unconsciously, nor do I want your attentions. That's a home truth for you, sir, and I'll thank you to take your hands off me."

They had reached the field now. The circling hawks were gone, not that Celia noticed.

To her surprise, the viscount did not appear at all upset by her stunning setdown, nor did he release her as she had demanded. Instead, he grinned down at her for a moment before he bent his head and kissed her square on the mouth.

She was so stunned, she did not react for a fateful time, something she was to chastise herself for later. Even, for one mad moment, she wanted to put her arms around his neck, pull him closer, kiss him back. Reason came to her better late than never, however, and she pulled away, breathing hard.

"It can be so much better, you know," he told her as if he knew that had been her first kiss. Celia wished the earth would swallow her up.

"But you must help. It is not enough to merely stand there like a statue. Sometimes it takes a kiss or two or three before one becomes adept at the art. For there is an art to love, ma'am. Yes, indeed, a definite art, one that must be cultivated carefully, learned thoroughly, and explored with abandon."

"I am not the least bit interested in such things. Let me pass," Celia demanded, trying to get by without touching him.

"I find it hard to believe that you, unlike other women, are not interested in love. Surely it is unnatural. But perhaps it is only that you have not encountered it yet? I am sure you would enjoy it if you gave it a chance."

Celia abandoned staring straight ahead to turn and face him. They had reached the woods again, and it was darker there, but there was still enough light for her to see his face clearly. He looked not only amused but at ease, and it angered her.

"You find it diverting to insult me, sir?" she demanded.

"But what could I have said that could be construed as an insult?" he asked, sounding puzzled. He thought Miss Anders had never looked so handsome, with those unusual eyes of hers flashing fire, and her color high. Even her chestnut hair seemed to crackle with energy like lightning on a hot summer night. Little curls of it had escaped her chignon, and he wondered how all of it would look flowing loose down her back.

"What you are suggesting we do—*I* do—is immoral. You should be ashamed of yourself."

"Why, what are you implying, ma'am?" he said. "You seem to think I have offered you a carte blanche, when no such invitation even occurred to me. Whatever you may think of me, ma'am, I *am a* gentleman, and I am very aware you are a lady. You are quite safe from my attentions, at least that way. I was merely discussing the subject of love philosophically."

Stung that he had once again put her in the wrong, and wounded, angry, and upset as well, Celia picked up her skirts and ran. It was a silly thing to do, and she knew it, for all the viscount had to do was mount his horse and come after her to catch her up again. But she had not been able to stand being in his company a moment longer, not aware as she was that in this encounter, yet once again, she had come out a poor second-best.

But what else could he have meant, prating of love as he had? she asked herself as she hurried down the ride. It was later than ever now. She'd be lucky to reach the castle before dark. Still, that was a bonus. It meant she could hide her hot face from the man behind her. She could hear the horse's hooves now. Obviously the viscount was not trying to catch her up, but maintaining a little distance a few paces to the rear. Indignant, Celia moved to one side of the path and waved her hand. "Go on," she said. "I do not want you following me."

"Come, ma'am, this is absurdly like a farce," he said easily. "You are making us both look ridiculous, and I do so dislike being made ridiculous."

Celia stamped her foot at him and made fists of her hands before she whirled and set off again, her head held high and her jaw tilted at the sky. Perhaps it was because in such a pose she could not

63

see where she was going that she suddenly tripped over a tree root that protruded from the ground. She did not fall as she cried out, for she had grasped the tree that caused the problem. Still, she could have wept, not from the pain of a twisted ankle, but from the chagrin she felt when she realized she had behaved like a silly, immature schoolgirl. What *must* he think of her?

The viscount was quick to dismount and come to her aid. "Which ankle?" he asked as he knelt before her.

"The left," Celia managed to say, swallowing her tears.

"Yes, you've twisted it finely. It is already swelling," he said as his hands, oddly gentle, inspected it. "You can't walk on it, that's certain."

Celia knew he spoke only the truth, for although she might be able to hobble a few steps, there was no way on earth she could get back to the castle unaided.

"I'll put you up before me. You must not worry because you do not ride. I'll keep you safe."

Celia nodded. She realized he was speaking to her just as he would speak to anyone in her same predicament. All trace of the teasing lover had disappeared, and she was more grateful to him than she could say.

She tried to ignore how his hands felt on her waist as he lifted her easily to the horse's back. Then she grasped the reins in terror. How very far it was to the ground! Suppose the horse decided to bolt! But a moment later the viscount was behind her, his arms coming around her to take the reins from her unresisting hands.

He set the horse to a walk so as not to jar her ankle, and he pulled her close against him. Much as Celia wanted to argue the position, she restrained herself. He was helping her; she was thankful for that at least.

As they left the bridle path and started down the drive, the low, fading sunlight painted long shadows on the grass and even deeper ones on the castle walls. It looked menacing somehow in the dimming light, and Celia shivered.

"Horrid, isn't it?" Drummond said. "I don't know how the duchess has stood it all these years. But stay! Perhaps you are cold? We'll soon be there."

When they arrived at the castle doors, a groom came running to take the horse. Drummond tossed him the reins and dismounted. Celia slid down into his waiting arms before the groom led the horse away. For a moment, William Welburn stared deep into her eyes. He saw the tears she was so desperately holding back, and he hugged her for a moment, to comfort her. Unfortunately, she misread the gesture and stiffened in indignation. The viscount sighed as he started up the steps. What ailed the woman? he asked himself. She was more prickly and difficult than any female he had ever encountered.

"You'll soon feel more the thing, Miss Anders," he said as he sounded the knocker. "You should soak that ankle, wrap it tightly to support it. I'm sure the housekeeper can help you. And may I suggest you have your dinner in your room, keep your weight off it until it is strong again?

"Ah, Bogle! Miss Anders has had an unfortunate accident. Please inform the duchess while I carry her to her room."

Only two people saw the viscount and Celia Anders come home that day, but both were extremely interested, leaning nearer their respective windows so as not to miss a single nuance of the occasion. It was noted that although Viscount Drummond spoke a few words, his companion did not reply. She seemed disturbed for some reason, as well as silent, although that could be due to the misfortune she appeared to have suffered.

The two who watched the viscount lift her from his horse wondered whether they had met by accident or design, and what they had been doing, and where. Long after the pair had been admitted to the castle, the onlookers were lost in conjecture.

William Welburn, fourth Viscount Drummond, and Miss Celia Anders, spinster—together? How very singular.

Six

CELIA FOLLOWED THE viscount's advice and remained secluded in her room that evening. To tell
the truth, she was feeling a little pulled even
though her ankle felt so much better after having
been soaked, rubbed with a special liniment, and
wrapped securely. Still, it was much more agreeable to be able to avoid the questions that were
sure to be asked about the accident. Let Viscount
Drummond deal with them. As a *gentleman* it was
the least he could do, and she would not have to
meet anyone's eyes until she had had a chance to
compose herself.

Remembering an embarrassing incident this very
evening made her blush, for she was sure she had
made a perfect cake of herself.

When the maid had brought in her dinner tray,
Celia had seen the bouquet on it, even from her position on the chaise across the room.

"I shall not accept those flowers," she said indig-
nantly. "The very idea! Take them with you when
you go."

"Miss?" the maid had asked, looking bewildered.
"But what am I to say to the duchess? She had
them sent up special for ye, from the conservatory.
That disappointed, she'll be."

"I—I am sorry," Celia blurted out, thinking rapidly. "In a confined space, flowers make me sneeze.

Please explain to the duchess and give her my thanks for her kindness."

What with that near disaster, and her smarting memories of the afternoon's complete rout at the viscount's hands, Celia was feeling a sincere lack of composure. Even, she told herself darkly, she wished she never had to go downstairs again. And then she shook her head at such silliness as she hopped her way to bed. It appeared to her that being almost thirty, and an adult of a great many years, was less than nothing if you were not used to society, and had little sophistication to call on to aid you. She might just as well be an untried girl for all the good her age had done for her.

By morning her ankle was much better. The swelling was almost gone, and it was the housekeeper's opinion that it would do no harm to walk on it as long as she did not overdo. Accordingly, after breakfast in bed, Celia dressed and spent the morning alone in the small salon, copying out play parts.

She was joined there shortly after nuncheon by Lady Powers, who was quick to express her surprise that Celia felt well enough to leave her bed. To Celia's relief, m'lady asked few questions about the accident, however, and was soon bent over her own papers. Still, as time went by, Celia wondered if she was feeling poorly, for she often frowned, or sighed a little. Perhaps her rheumatism was bothering her, or she had a headache, Celia thought when she saw Lady Powers massage her temples.

David Powers joined them a short time later, and Celia was glad to see his mother's eyes brighten when he came in.

"Since I have only the butler's part in this play we are to do, I thought I might help you with your penmanship, ladies," he said, his eyes twinkling as he took a seat. "Besides, if I linger in the hall much longer, watching how Bogle, er, *butles,* I'm afraid I shall make him uneasy."

Lady Powers laughed. "Not a bit of it, David. He's probably delighted you have come to the source, and has added a great many flourishes to his already august performance for your benefit."

She gave him the villain's part to copy, and only the scratching of three quills was heard in the small salon for some time.

But eventually, a footman came in with a note for Celia. She paled a little as he presented the tray, and wished the Powerses were not sitting there with her when she opened it. Of course, they both bent industriously to their work to give her privacy, but she was conscious of them even so.

It was a short note of only a few lines, and it was, as she had feared, from Viscount Drummond.

"My dear Miss Anders," he began. "Since it is not raining, nor even threatening to, I invite you to join me for a drive at three. The fresh air will do us both good. I shall be waiting before the castle at that hour. If you do not appear, I shall know it was only cowardice that kept you from obliging, for I have it on very good authority that you have been up and about all day."

As Celia tucked the note away in her pocket, she prayed her heightened breathing was not too evident and that she had her features under firm control. William Welburn might call her a coward as much as he pleased; she had no intention of joining him, not this day, or any other.

Suddenly, Celia remembered the amusements the dowager duchess had listed for her guests, and she wrote some notes of her own.

When three o'clock came, she was in the front hall clad in a light pelisse, and a dashing new bonnet she had been saving for the first fine day. With her were Harriet Hadley, Bartholomew Whitaker, and Duke Ainsworth.

The dowager's landau was waiting for them when they left the castle. Beyond it, Viscount Drummond waited, his small tiger at his team's heads. As Celia stole a glance at him, the viscount bowed, making a grand gesture with his top hat. To her disgust, he did not appear to be at all chagrined, for his smile was wide and he was obviously amused.

His phaeton passed the landau as Celia's party was taking their seats, and it bowled up the drive at a fast clip. Celia set herself to chatting with the others, although she couldn't help but think that a drive in such a smart vehicle as the phaeton was much to be preferred over the dowager's landau. Or she did until she remembered who was driving it.

That evening she found that a twisted ankle meant there was little she could do to avoid company she did not care for. She was tied to a seat in the drawing room before dinner, and after it as well, at the mercy of anyone who happened by. First it was Mrs. Grey, whispering more venom in her ear. She was followed by Drusilla Dawkins, who had a whole day's worth of clever things Charity had said or done to report. And after dinner Lord Drummond trapped her there.

The musicians from Westbridge had arrived, and the carpet had been rolled up for dancing. Celia was content to sit and watch the others on this occasion, although she wished the viscount had not been so attentive.

He asked if she had enjoyed her drive that afternoon; she said it had been delightful. He told her he hoped she would soon be dancing again, for he intended to beg the first waltz; she announced she

70

did not care to waltz. He wondered if she had had any further trouble finding her way about the castle; she informed him she was taking the greatest care, as she had discovered how truly unsavory losing your way could be.

Since their entire conversation went that way, Celia was sure Lord Drummond must have been relieved when her uncle Dudley came and ousted him from his place beside her. Perhaps he had formed a disgust for her and would avoid her in the future? Celia told herself it would be a tremendous relief if such a thing should happen.

She could not know how amused William Welburn was as he strolled away toward the dowager's chair. He thought Miss Anders like an enraged kitten, desperately fighting a much stronger opponent with only sharp little claws she was just beginning to know how to employ. Really, he had not expected such fun from this house party, he thought as he bowed to his hostess and took the seat beside her.

Dolly Farrington had seen him in attendance on Miss Anders, and she thanked him for his kindness. "For I know very well Celia Anders could not possibly appeal to you, William," she added, touching his hand for a moment in approval. "And I never expected you to show such good manners. Generally, as you know, you do only what you please."

He smiled down at her. "How very unkind of you to remind me, and you my godmother, too. But to be truthful, I find Miss Anders a delight."

"You do?" the dowager asked, her eyes wide. "Why?"

"Well, she is so different from the other women I generally meet," he said slowly, as if he were searching for reasons this particular one appealed to him so. "She is so starched up and moral, for instance. And . . ."

"Here now, William, you've not been making love to the girl, have you? For I won't have it, do you hear me?"

Drummond held up one big, well-manicured hand. "No need to fly up into the boughs, ma'am," he said easily. "I am only teasing her."

"Yes, of course you are, but have you ever thought she might not understand what you are about? She has been little in society. She does not know our ways. And it would be cruel to hurt her."

"I won't hurt her. What can you be thinking, ma'am?" he said sharply. "I'll only give her something to remember when she returns to her home in London. Really, you know, you might have a little more faith in me."

The dowager looked as if she were going to say a great deal more, but Lord Manchester was bowing before her and asking her to join the set that was forming, and she was forced to go away. But she did not forget what Lord Drummond had said, and often during the rest of the evening she looked at Celia Anders, puzzled.

The young woman was attractive, of course, but not the beauty the viscount had always preferred. And although her gown was in style and pretty, it was not in the first mode of elegance, something her godson would notice and regret at once. Truly, Dolly Farrington did not see what attracted him, and she promised herself she would spend quite a bit more time with Celia Anders to find out what it was. For it would be truly unfortunate, indeed she could almost say disastrous, if anything were to come of this, even if it were only to be a desperate flirtation and a few stolen kisses. *Truly* unfortunate! And by inviting them both to her party, she

72

would be the one at fault. Society would not forgive her for that.

In spite of the viscount's sparring, Celia enjoyed that evening. The music was gay, and she liked watching the couples dancing. She saw Lord Manchester and Lady Powers taking part in a set, and spending the best part of another one deep in conversation on a sofa against the far wall. Mrs. Grey caught her eye and nodded wisely, and Celia felt as if she had been caught peeking behind the closed curtains of a private room.

Then there was David Powers's visit beside her. How he did make her laugh! And Duke Ainsworth's progress around the room. He asked every lady to dance, showing off his kind manners, and he was graceful in performance, although Celia would have sworn he was not the type. Bartholomew Whitaker was less obliging. He sat with Celia for some time, making idle conversation, and seldom danced.

When she went up to bed on her uncle's arm, Celia almost felt as if she were part of a large family. It was so comfortable, knowing there would always be others to converse with, especially after all the times she had eaten dinner silently with an uncle so deep in a problem of his own he had forgotten her very existence. And if some members of this "family" were not as pleasant as others, well, wasn't that true of real-life families as well?

Later, just as she was about to climb into bed, Harriet Hadley knocked on her door. She begged a few minutes of Celia's time, and, intrigued, Celia bade her enter.

Miss Hadley was flushed a wild rose color which Celia thought became her, but her gray eyes were full of tears that threatened to overflow at any moment.

"But what is it, Miss Hadley?" Celia asked when they were both seated.

"Oh, it is so horrid! I did not know where to turn! But although we do not know each other very well, I sense you are kind, and you can advise me. There is no one else here. Besides, I don't know who is spreading these tales about me."

"What tales?" Celia asked, remembering Mrs. Grey's delight in scandal.

"My maid has heard the most terrible gossip about me," Miss Hadley said in a desperate whisper. Celia had to lean closer to hear her.

"It is all over the servants' hall. And how soon will it be before it reaches the dowager's ears, indeed, everyone's here? I am twenty-one now! There must be no scandal, for this Season I have to find a husband. My father said . . ."

She fell silent, hiding her face in her handkerchief.

"But what is the gossip?" Celia asked to give her time to recover. "I have heard nothing."

Miss Hadley lowered the handkerchief, looking a little more at ease. "Someone has started a rumor that I take things that don't belong to me and that no one's possessions are safe. It is true I absent-mindedly put a pair of sugar tongs in my reticule a few days ago. I was thinking of something else at the time, and I was astounded when I found them there a bit later. Of course I returned them at once."

She paused and stared at Celia, as if to gauge whether she was believed or not. "You do think I am telling the truth, don't you, Miss Anders?" she asked desperately. "I tell you on my honor, it is just as I have said. And surely you yourself have put things in strange places, haven't you?"

Celia could not remember doing so, but she nodded and made soothing noises.

"But who could it be who would say such terrible things about me?" Miss Hadley demanded. "Who could dislike me so much that they would make mischief this way? I have done nothing I know of to inspire such enmity."

She paused then, her eyes narrowing. Celia waited.

"Do you think it could be one or both of the Flowers twins?" her visitor asked at last. "I know it sounds far-fetched, but perhaps they do not want me here, taking some of the gentlemen's attention from themselves. For of course there are only Earl Castleton and Viscount Drummond as possible suitors."

"Because they have titles? But what of Charles Danforth? Mr. Whitaker and Mr. Ainsworth?" Celia asked, intrigued.

"Well, of course a title is to be preferred, but all those men are from excellent families. It is not that," Miss Hadley said, shaking her head. "But Mr. Danforth has no fortune, and he is a poet. No sensible father would consider his suit for a moment. Mr. Whitaker thinks we are all of us only silly young things, and Mr. Ainsworth is going to remain a bachelor for the rest of his life."

She seemed to see some question in Celia's eyes, for she added, "I do assure you I am right, Miss Anders. Duke Ainsworth is all kindness and attention, but there will be no commitment. He is too comfortable as he is to want a wife to disturb his peace. One of my uncles is just like him.

"But who can it be who is trying to ruin me?" she asked, recalling her primary concern in a rush.

"I have no idea," Celia admitted. "It is so vicious, it makes me shiver."

"Perhaps I should go away. Pretend I have been called back to London suddenly. My great-aunt is ill; it would not be such a terrible lie."

"No, you must not leave," Celia told her. "That would imply there was truth to the rumor and you were running away from it. I think you must stay and face down the gossip."

"It is easy enough for you to say so. No one is talking about you," Miss Hadley said, looking indignant.

"No, they aren't. But there has been conjecture about two others in the party. And the gossip about them is quite as distasteful as the talk about you," Celia told her.

She wished she had not spoken, when Miss Hadley edged forward on her chair. "Who is it?" she breathed. "What is being said?"

Celia shook her head. "I won't repeat it. That only plays into the hands of the one who is doing all this." When she saw the disappointment writ large on her visitor's face, she added, "Surely you can understand why, being a victim yourself. But tell me, don't you think these things could have begun with the servants? They are such gossips, are they not?"

"Yes," Miss Hadley said slowly. "But if that were the case, my maid would know how it started. I asked her about it myself. She says it came out all at once. One meal no one said anything about me; the next it was all around the table. It was impossible for her to pin it down to only one person."

She shuddered. "How awful it is to know that *servants* are discussing you! To think they call me—*me*—thief! I cannot look a single one of them in the eye without cringing."

"Yes, it must be terrible for you, but you must overcome it," Celia was quick to say. For several more minutes she lectured Miss Hadley on the best way to go on, and when the door closed behind the girl at last, she said a small prayer that her advice had been sound.

For what did she know of such things? she asked herself as she climbed into bed. She was only guessing in her desire to help. But perhaps there was something else she could do to solve the little mystery of who was spreading rumors.

She decided to give it a great deal of thought on the morrow, when she was not so tired.

Seven

*E*ARLY THE FOLLOWING afternoon, Lady Cassandra found Dolly Farrington alone in one of the drawing rooms and took a seat beside her. In the great hall beyond they could hear the play being rehearsed. It was only a distant rumble of voices, but the noise made Lady Cassandra say, "It was a brilliant idea of yours, Dolly, to think of giving a play. The young people in the party were getting restless."

The dowager agreed. "Yes, and that's when trouble is brewed. I thought to keep them occupied until the weather clears. If it ever does," she added gloomily, for the afternoon was blustery again, with frequent showers.

"It is very true that the devil finds work for idle hands," Lady Cassandra remarked, taking out the fringe she was knotting and setting to work.

Her friend laughed. "How pious you sound, Cassie! But I can recall a time when you were not so prim and proper. Do you remember the masquerade Lady Foulkner gave when we were girls? And what we did there?"

Lady Cassandra dropped her fringe in her agitation. "Dolly, not a word! Not a single word if you love me."

She thought for a moment before she added, "Do you know, I never told Henry about that, not in all the years we were married. Do you think that was wrong of me?"

"Why? It happened before you met him, goose," the dowager told her.

"Well, yes, but surely there should be no secrets between husband and wife."

"How betwaddled you sound, Cassie. Of course there are secrets. I imagine Henry had a number he kept from you. He would not have been a man if he hadn't."

When she saw the slightly distressed look her friend assumed, she wished she had held her tongue.

"What secrets could he have had?" Lady Cassandra demanded. "What do you mean?"

She sounded so perturbed that Dolly was quick to say she had only been teasing, for of course dear Henry had been a living saint. But deep inside she was sure she was right. Good heavens, if everyone told their spouse everything, what a piece of work there would be. And nary a single happy marriage in the entire kingdom as a result. But then, the dowager thought as she smoothed her embroidery, Cassie had ever been an idealist.

She was reminded of Celia Anders, and she frowned a little. From what she could see, that young lady was the soul of practicality. Dolly Farrington wondered if her uncle had been honest with her, or had he kept the facts of her birth one of those secrets she and Cassie had just been discussing. Knowing how men tended to ignore unpleasant things, the dowager was sure Miss Anders had no idea of her background. Pray it would remain a secret.

"You are looking a little disturbed, Dolly. Is something troubling you?" Lady Cassandra asked, interrupting her musing.

"I am not sure," the dowager said, lowering her voice and looking around as if to make sure they were completely alone. "Perhaps I am making 'much ado about nothing.' I do not know. But I only did it to give the poor dear a treat. If anything bad results from that, I shall never forgive myself."

"Who are you talking about? Someone here at your party?"

"Celia Anders. I met her last spring when Reginald would insist on stopping to call on Dudley Bell in London. I was sure I would be bored, but it was no such thing. Miss Anders welcomed me, served tea, and we had a charming conversation. She was such a delightful creature that I felt sorry for her, as good as buried with her bookish uncle, and never going anywhere, or having a bit of fun. Poor, poor dear! So, of course, when Reginald asked me to invite Mr. Bell here during the party, I had the brilliant idea that Miss Anders would enjoy it as well."

"I am sure she is doing so. How very like you to think of her, Dolly. But what is there about the situation that causes you concern?"

"My godson, Drummond," the dowager said in dire tones.

"William Welburn? What about him?"

"I saw him carrying Miss Anders into the castle after she twisted her ankle. His expression as he did so, just the way he bent his head over hers, made me uneasy. And so last night I taxed him with it, in a very subtle way, of course. He admitted he is treating Miss Anders to a whirlwind flirtation. She is very innocent for all her age, and I fear may think him in earnest. I would not have her hurt.

"Oh, William says he will not hurt her, but what do men know of the matter, I ask you that, Cassie? The poor thing is apt to leave here bereft, to fall into a deep decline."

Her companion made a distressed noise as the dowager went on. "But that is not all, horrid as it is. I am living in dread that *he* will fall in love with *her*. It is just the unsuitable thing men are so prone to do. And never having succumbed to any eligible young lady all these years might make William more susceptible. But a union between him and Miss Anders is not to be considered."

"Whyever not?" Lady Cassandra asked, her eyes wide and her fringe quite forgotten.

Looking around again, the dowager leaned closer and spoke for some time. Her friend listened intently, her face showing disbelief, distaste, and finally horror.

"Oh, no, it would never do, not for Drummond," she said when the dowager's tale was told. "Surely it would have been better not to have asked her here, Dolly, but it is too late for that. But perhaps you are just imagining the viscount's attraction? It might be only as he says, that he is setting her up as his flirt to pass the time. I do not think he will overstep the line, for he is, in spite of his rakish ways, a gentleman. Look on the bright side, my dear, do."

Dolly sighed and picked up her handwork again. "I promise I shall try to, Cassie. If only I could be sure William will not do something outrageous. I have never understood him, you know, love him though I do. I never did, even when he was a child. But if things get out of hand, I shall speak to him again.

"How sad it is that men become so indignant when they are scolded and advised for their own good. There's not a one of 'em who can be reasoned with, not when they are being taken to task."

Lady Cassandra took exception to this sweeping statement, giving examples from her dealings with her late husband. Her Grace contradicted her, and the subject of Celia Anders and Viscount Drummond was forgotten.

Several minutes later, Bogle came in to inform his mistress that a contretemps had developed between the chef and some of his underlings, and she went away to the kitchens to deal with it. She was very fond of the dishes the Frenchman sent up to her table, and she intended to lure him away to the dower house when the time came she would be free to leave the castle. But nothing must be allowed to upset his genius until then.

Lady Cassandra left the room as well. She planned to spend some time with her niece-in-law, who she could tell was in a state of almost constant indignation that her little daughter was being royally snubbed by one and all.

Lady Cassandra sighed. She had tried to tell Drusilla how it would be, but the woman was dense when it came to her only child. Her aunt could not look forward to their coming encounter, and would have foregone it completely if she had not felt it was her duty, after bringing the two of them with her, to see to their welfare every day.

Charity Dawkins waited a very long time before she climbed down from the large wing chair at the end of the drawing room, where she had been seated, hidden from sight. Her legs were stiff from being folded under her for such a length of time, but she ignored them. As always when she was roaming about the castle, she had a book with her, although she rarely opened it. It was only a ploy she could use if she were caught somewhere she should not be, listening.

She had heard all the silly things grown-ups said about children. "Little pitchers have big ears" was just one of them. And sometimes grown-ups spelled out words of warning, as if she had never learned to spell. How stupid they were!

But never had her eavesdropping been as successful as it had been today. Why, the story she had heard was almost too good to be true! And when it came out, what a hullabaloo there would be. And she would make sure it did come out, she told herself as she went to the door and stood there, listening. When not a sound disturbed the silence, she let herself out of the drawing room, closed the door softly, and hurried away.

She, too, had seen Viscount Drummond cuddling Miss Anders when they came back to the castle together riding double, and she had wondered how she could use the incident to her advantage.

It was not that she had anything against Miss Anders, for outside of ignoring her, as everyone did, she had done nothing. But that Viscount Drummond—well! Staring at her as if she were some disgusting insect, sneering at her. He'd pay for that. She'd make sure of it, just see if she didn't.

So there was no way this wonderful tidbit would stay a secret. But she would not reveal it right away. She wanted to savor it by herself for a while. Really, she told herself as she sidled by the elderly butler to go upstairs to her room, life was getting so interesting, she could hardly bear it.

Bogle sniffed as she went by him, but today Charity barely noticed, for she was deep in thought.

That footman who had thrown her out of the breakfast room, well, he could have told people how unwise it was to cross Charity Dawkins—if he had known she was the cause of his broken leg, that is. She had taken an almost unholy delight in fastening the twine across one of the steps when she knew he would be using the back stairs shortly. And in the to-do there had been immediately after, it had been a small matter to cut the twine and leave it dangling by the side of the stairs until it had been safe to remove it. She hadn't worried about being suspected. No one thought a child could do anything. More fools they.

Charity giggled as she let herself into her room and closed the door behind her. That Lord Manchester would have thought twice about telling her to make herself scarce if he had known she had been the one to tell about his trips through the halls late at night. Of course, she had not seen that for herself, but she had heard one of the guests' valets telling another in an aside one afternoon in the servants' hall when she had been there with her mother's maid for tea. And it had been a small matter to get Mary to tell the other maids about it, and from them a small step to their mistresses' ears.

But she had seen Miss Hadley pocket the sugar tongs. True, the blonde had called attention to what she had done as soon as she discovered it, but that had not kept Charity from using the incident to call Miss Hadley a thief. Miss Hadley had been improvident enough to tell the Flowers twins she thought Charity was positively weird. No one called Charity Dawkins names and got away with it! No one.

And she intended to repay everyone at the castle who had been mean to her. Mama was right. These people had no manners. It would serve them right.

Of course, the person who was the most to blame, and who was really going to pay for it, was the Dowager Duchess of Wentworth. When you came to think of it, it was all *her* fault. If she had only allowed Charity to join the party, everyone else would have had to go along with her. It was her castle, wasn't it? But the dowager had not done that. Charity was almost sorry she had used the twine on the footman. The dowager was so old, she would probably die if she fell down a flight of stairs, and it would serve her right if she did.

But something else would occur to her. It always had, right from the time she was eight and she had poisoned Mary Booth's puppies because the little girl would not give her even one for her very own.

Indeed, although Mrs. Dawkins looked at her child through rose-colored glasses, there were those in Northumberland who had their suspicions about her. They could have warned the dowager and her guests that it was foolish to turn your back on Charity Dawkins, or allow her to hear any information you did not want the world to know. And it was most unwise to speak of her in a demeaning way if you knew what was good for you.

Reminded of the butler's sniff, Charity went to her desk and took out her notebook to put another tick against Bogle's name. The day was coming, she promised herself as she counted the many ticks he had accumulated. He would not escape either.

Shortly after breakfast that day, Earl Castleton had assembled his cast to begin rehearsing the play.

Her copying chores completed, Celia was asked to serve as prompter. From the stumbling attempts made by the actors, she could see the prompter was going to be a very important person. Of course, no one was sure of their entrances and exits, and with the exception of Mr. Grey, they were still reading their parts. That surly gentleman was playing Miss Hadley's elderly father, and Celia hoped Earl Castleton would not change a bit of his performance. He had every line memorized, and his shouted abuse, his indignation and scorn, were perfect for the part. Of course, she told herself when they stopped for a rest, Mr. Grey was only playing himself, but what a success he was at it.

His wife had been cast as the parlor maid, and he seemed to take special delight in shouting at her. Completely flustered, Mrs. Grey dropped her feather duster a number of times.

Since Celia had no prompting to do as yet, she amused herself by rating everyone's performance. She thought Viscount Drummond needed to put quite a bit more animation into his role before he could be said to be the perfect villain. But perhaps he was saving himself for later?

Charles Danforth complained that his lines had been written badly, and bragged about how much better he could have done the play. When the earl managed to get him to attend to business, he was no more heroic than the viscount was villainous. As his friend in the play, Bartholomew Whitaker managed to keep a straight face even when the Flowers twins giggled both onstage and off. Celia told herself she was very bad to be looking forward so eagerly to their collective demise early in the third act.

Miss Hadley was very pale today, as if she had not slept well. Her reading was wooden. Celia was reminded that she must do some serious thinking about that young lady's problem.

But who could have been spreading rumors about her? she wondered. The same person who had told everyone about Lord Manchester's and Lady Powers's affair? But *why*?

Celia was aware that most of the guests had known each other before their arrival at the castle, and if they did not all appear to be the best of friends—only casual acquaintances—at least she had noted no enmity among them. And surely the dowager would not have invited people who were at daggers drawn, lest they ruin everyone else's stay at the castle.

Perhaps the guilty party was Mrs. Grey? Celia had seen how much delight the woman took in gossiping. Why, she could be considered the prime suspect. She did not seem to have any other interests. The Greys were childless, and outside of a rather ugly altar cloth Mrs. Grey was embroidering, she did nothing else, neither read nor sketch nor play the pianoforte.

But somehow, in spite of everything pointing a finger at the woman, Celia found herself thinking she was almost too perfect for the part. And the talk that was going around was more than just gossip. There was a tiny vindictive edge to it that made Celia shiver. And, she told herself, although Mrs. Grey was fond of scandal, she was only shallow, not mean. Or so it seemed to her. However, she was aware that in an unromantic world, people like Mrs. Grey could well be more than they appeared.

Later, after she had seen the twins whispering to each other and looking at Miss Hadley, Celia made a point of going in to nuncheon with her.

The gentlemen had scattered to their own pursuits; Celia wondered if they had heard the gossip, and what they thought of it. She wished she could have asked Bartholomew Whitaker. He seemed a sensible man, perhaps he could have advised her. But she did not know if he knew of the talk, and she did not want to be the one to enlighten him if he should be in the dark. As she took a serving of spiced beef, she reminded herself she was in a very awkward position.

Before some others came in and conversation became general, Celia was only able to whisper a few words of encouragement to the tormented Miss Hadley.

When they both left the room with Lady Powers, they came upon Charity Dawkins in the hall. The little girl had a book under her arm, and Celia tried to smile at her. She wondered at the way Charity looked so steadily at them all. Surely the child did not know the talk that was going around, did she? It was all of it most unsuitable for a little girl.

Miss Hadley excused herself to go to her room so she could study her part in the play. Celia hoped that was her real reason, and not that she intended to cower in seclusion there. Lady Powers drifted away as well.

For herself, Celia intended to curl up somewhere and read. She had returned the late duke's stud book the day she had taken it from the library, and now she was immersed in one of Walter Scott's novels.

She did not go to the library. Others were sure to be there and she would be drawn into conversation. Instead, she went to the small salon where she and Lady Powers had spent so much time copying parts. As she had hoped, a small fire was burning in the grate, and the room was quite empty. Happily, Celia found her place and was soon deep in her book.

Eight

"So THIS IS where you've hidden yourself away, Miss Anders," Viscount Drummond said cheerfully as he entered the room a long time later. Celia jumped and dropped her book.

As he bent to retrieve it, he said, "I do seem to make a habit of startling you, don't I? I don't mean to, you know. And we must hope that today's meeting will not result in any twisted ankles, must we not? I am glad to see you have recovered so well from the first one.

"What are you reading? Ah, *The Lady of the Lake*. Are you enjoying it?"

"Very much so," Celia said on her best behavior and determined to be pleasant.

"And you wish I would go away so you could continue to do so," he added as he took a seat across from her. He grinned at her as he continued. "What a shame it is I have never been able to take the hint, you know. Something must have been lacking in my upbringing."

Celia looked only mildly interested, for she had set a guard on her tongue. As if he knew how tested she was, he laughed at her.

"Speaking of upbringings, may I ask you about yours, ma'am?"

"What do you want to know?" she asked, her brow furrowed at this abrupt change of subject.

She was not at all sure she wanted to discuss such a thing with him. It was too personal.

"Well, it seems passing strange to me that your uncle should have been the one to bring you up. Didn't you have any aunts or female cousins to do the job? In my experience, everyone's family is positively littered with such good ladies. At least mine is."

"I know very little of my family," Celia admitted. "I know only that my mother died shortly after my birth and my uncle Dudley raised me from that time."

"Perhaps you were a very naughty little girl and it was thought a man might be able to handle you better?" he suggested, wondering where her father had been, and her father's family.

Celia stared at him. "I was a very good little girl," she said.

"And, I have no doubt, you are a good girl still," he said.

She turned to gaze into the fire, to avoid his knowing look.

He chuckled as he went to a table set against the wall to pour them both a glass of wine.

He might have asked if I cared for one, Celia thought resentfully as she was forced to take the glass he brought her.

"I have heard from the gardener that tomorrow promises to be fair. If it should be so, the dowager is getting up a party to go to Bath for the day. Would you be interested in such an outing?"

"Oh, yes, indeed," Celia said, smiling now. "I have longed to see Bath, the Abbey and the Pump Room, and I never thought to have the chance."

"Splendid. I shall do myself the honor of driving you there." He paused before he went on. "Do not deny me, if you please. Only consider that by going with me behind my chestnuts, you will arrive in Bath long before any of the others, and so will have more opportunity to explore it."

Celia shook her head. "You are the most domineering man," she said, her voice wondering. "Do you always get your own way, sir?"

"Most of the time," he admitted cheerfully. "And a good thing, too. I become extremely testy when I do not. And any one of my acquaintances, to say nothing of my servants, could tell you that that is a state to be avoided at all cost."

"I suspect you have been royally spoiled all your life, perhaps even subject to temper tantrums as a child. How unfortunate it is your parents were not stricter with you."

"I assure you they were, ma'am. But my mother often remarked how very like my father I was. An inherited trait, you see, not one that could be easily reversed.

"Tell me, do you think this play we are attempting has any chance of success? I saw you watching us all so carefully this morning."

"Well, of course, Mr. Grey is magnificent," Celia told him. Drummond admired the little smile that quivered on her lips. "As for the rest, perhaps when they have learned their lines and can be free to look about and move as well they will do better. Everyone is rather tentative at the moment."

"Including me?"

"Including you. You are nowhere near as menacing as a villain should be."

"Perhaps I hesitated to frighten the ladies. I do assure you I can be as menacing as I can be testy. But I am sure you must agree it is difficult to completely change one's personality. Especially if one is *very* good-natured and has such a *lovable* disposition."

As Celia chuckled, he grinned. Then his expression changed.

"Tell me another thing, Miss Anders. Have you heard the gossip that is going around? What do you make of it?"

"So you have heard it, too. Do all the men know?"

"I imagine so, although we have not sat down together to discuss it, of course. But the Powers-Manchester affair was no surprise. They have been in love with each other for years, and most people in the ton know it. In fact I'm sure my godmother invited them here so they could be together. She is all kindness, don't you agree?"

When Celia had no answer, he went on smoothly. "I am a little surprised Mrs. Grey is overset by what she must know is very old news. But perhaps it seems worse in the intimate setting of a house party. As for Miss Hadley being a thief, I find that hard to believe."

"I do not think she is," Celia said. "She came to me to ask my advice. She was so upset and confused, for she has no idea who would say such a scurrilous thing about her."

He nodded, looking thoughtful. "I wonder who will be next?"

"You think the gossip will continue? Why?"

"Why not? When someone enjoys making mischief in such a way, they are not likely to be satisfied with only two victims. No, the more success they have at stirring things up and bewildering people, the longer they will continue."

"Then we have only to wait until everyone but one has been maligned to discover the culprit," Celia said. "I do not think it will be a pleasant time, however. Oh, I do wish all of this would stop."

The viscount finished his wine and put the empty glass down on the table beside him. "Yes, it is unfortunate. And very mysterious, too. I have known these people all my life. I cannot imagine them spreading rumors about their peers. It is incongruous."

"You do not know me. Or my uncle," Celia reminded him.

For a moment there was silence in the small salon, and Celia did not lower her eyes as Drummond studied her face, his own face serious. "No," he said at last. "It is true I do not know you well, but I cannot imagine you doing such a thing. Your eyes are too honest."

Before she could thank him, he went on. "I have to wonder, though, what will be said about you, Miss Anders."

"And about you, m'lord," came the quick retort as Celia rose and curtsied. The viscount walked with her to the door. Just as they reached it, Charity Dawkins went by in the hall, and he grimaced.

"Does that annoying child do nothing but roam the castle?" he asked before she was quite out of earshot. "I seem to bump into her everywhere I turn, and most unpleasant the experience is, too."

"Shh, she will hear you," Celia admonished him. "And it is really not her fault. There is no one here for her to talk to. She must be lonesome."

"Then let that besotted mother of hers keep her company. She's nutty enough about her," he said sternly.

"What a blessing it is you have never married and had children, sir," Celia was quick to say. "I do not think you would make a good father."

"Of course I would," he told her, taking her hand and holding it tightly in his so she could not escape. "One is always more tolerant of one's own brats, isn't that so? Witness Mrs. Dawkins."

Celia pulled her hand from his and made her escape. As she went down the hall, he called after

93

her, "Do not forget our appointment to go to Bath together, Miss Anders. As I've told you, you are a delightful conversationalist. I'm looking forward to having you quite to myself both going and coming."

Celia did not take a deep breath until she was safely around the next corner. She did not have to turn back to know Drummond was smiling and looking very pleased with himself. But she had no intention of giving up the treat of seeing Bath at last. And if that meant she had to endure the viscount's company, she would do so gladly. But in truth, she told herself, smiling a little now, she was not at all loathe to do so. It was only that she felt she must display a conventional reluctance that made her protest. She was beginning to like Viscount Drummond. She admitted it, if only to herself. Of course, sometimes he was maddening, but when he was behaving himself, he was a pleasant companion and a gentleman. And now she would have the chance to sit behind that matchless team, being whisked to Bath in the greatest of style. Perhaps there was some romance left in the world after all?

Should she wear her new leaf green carriage dress and its matching bonnet? Or would her Devonshire brown pelisse over her jonquil gown be more attractive? She hurried to her room to inspect them so she could decide, and as she did so, she prayed tomorrow would be fair.

Other couples spent some time together that afternoon.

Lady Powers and Lord Manchester visited the north gallery, supposedly to admire the castle's vast collection of landscapes and portraits but in reality to discuss their predicament in a location where they could be quite alone and without fear of interruption.

"I do not understand why you are so distraught, Louisa," Lord Manchester said as he held her close in his arms. "Surely you know our love for each other has been common knowledge for years."

"Yes, that is so," Lady Powers admitted softly. "And yet I had hoped my son would never learn of it. I have been so careful to keep it from him, at least. But now, here in the castle, how can he avoid hearing what people are saying about his mother? His *mother*, Alastair! It is for him I weep."

Lord Manchester handed her his snowy handkerchief and made soothing noises. He was sure David Powers was well aware of his mother's love for a man who was not his father, and had been for years. But if it made Louisa happier to think he did not, he would not disillusion her.

He had loved Louisa Bradley Powers for a very long time. Indeed, he had fallen in love with her when she first came to London for the Season. But her father had forced her to a marriage with the wealthy Viscount Powers, and as an obedient daughter she had had to bow to his decree. However, the minute Powers's heir was born, she had left him, to live alone with her child.

Lord Manchester did not know what hold Louisa had over her husband that he would accept such a situation, for she had never told him. But it must have been of great magnitude, or Viscount Powers would never have agreed to the separation.

She had insisted Lord Manchester keep their love a secret for many years, for nothing must happen that might take her beloved son from her. He was forced to agree. He had never married, nor did he intend to until that happy day Viscount Powers was carried to his grave and he was free to claim his Louisa at last.

Remembering their tortured yet blissful history,

Alastair Manchester touched Louisa's cheek tenderly and bent to kiss her and whisper that everything would be all right.

The other couple met inadvertently. Hurrying to her room, Harriet Hadley had rounded a corner and stumbled right into Earl Castleton. Only a short time ago she would have been on her knees in gratitude for such an opportunity, but now tears of chagrin streamed down her cheeks.

"Miss Hadley, forgive me! Have I hurt you?" the earl asked as he grasped her upper arms to steady her.

"No, oh, please, let me go," she whispered.

Seeing her despair, Jaspar Howland wanted nothing so much as to do just that, but something kept him from releasing her. Putting an arm around her waist, he led her to a nearby room. As he pushed her gently down on a sofa and took the seat beside her, he said, "You are distraught. I will stay with you until you feel more the thing."

Miss Hadley covered her face with her handkerchief and sobbed in her distress. Tentatively, the earl put his arm around her again and drew her close to pat her on the back.

"There, there," he said awkwardly, wondering why it had been his bad luck to have been in the hall just then. "I am sure whatever it is is nowhere near as bad as you think, ma'am. But never mind. Cry all you like. It might make you feel better."

Miss Hadley did not appear to hear him, but she managed to turn his beautifully tied cravat into a limp, damp travesty of a gentleman's neckwear only a short time later.

"I say, it's not this gossip that's been going around about you that's making you so sad, is it?"

Miss Hadley moaned and buried her face deeper into his neck.

"But no one believes such a thing," he assured her, raising his head to escape her burrowing. It was beginning to tickle, and he hardly thought his breaking into gales of laughter would do anything to ease the situation. "Why, everyone has been saying it would be impossible for *you* to steal. On my honor. Word of a Howland."

She gave a little hiccup. Sensing she was growing calmer, he went on. "You must not let this overset you, indeed you must not. That is just to play into the hands of whoever started the talk. You must appear to be above such scandal, smile, and look calm. Then you will foil that person and they will have to stop spreading rumors about you."

"But—but everyone *knows,*" Miss Hadley moaned. "How can I pretend nothing is wrong?"

The earl thought there was no way she could, not if she were to break down in tears every time someone looked at her sideways, but he did not say so. Women, as he knew, were sensitive creatures, made to be cherished and protected even when that was the last thing on earth you wanted to do. So he would do what he could for Miss Hadley short of marrying her.

"But this will soon be very stale news," he told her, drawing back a little and releasing her. Lord, if anyone should come in, or even go by this room, he'd be in the suds! "I'm sure there'll be more gossip about someone else shortly, and everyone will have forgotten all about you."

"What gossip? About who?" she demanded, raising her head to stare at him. He tried not to shudder, for Miss Hadley did not cry prettily. The tip of her nose was bright red, her face was blotchy, and her eyes were swollen.

"Well, there has already been talk about Lord Manchester and Lady Powers. Surely there will be others maligned. Why, I myself might very well be accused of being involved in a breech of promise suit, the way things have been going."

"Have you been?" she gasped. "I mean, were you?"

"Of course not," the earl said, annoyed. "I was only giving a hypothetical example of what might happen."

"Oh, I see," Miss Hadley said, drooping again. Castleton suspected it was from disappointment she had not discovered what a cad he was, and for a moment he was tempted to regale her with a fictional lurid past.

That strange little girl he had seen wandering around more than once came by the door just then and paused to stare at them. Something about her pale blue eyes and expressionless face made him uneasy. He rose quickly and excused himself.

Surely he had done everything he could to assist Miss Hadley, he told himself. Now he intended to find his cousin Bart and ask him why either one of them had agreed to come to this tiresome, horrible house party.

Nine

THE VISCOUNT AND Celia Anders arrived in Bath shortly after ten the following morning.

Celia had awakened with the dawn, and she said a prayer of thanks when she saw the day would be fine.

The various carriages needed had been called for nine, but it was doubtful that with so many interested in the excursion to assemble, they would actually be able to start out at that time.

Celia tried not to look self-conscious seated beside Drummond, his diminutive tiger up behind, but she was aware everyone's eyes were on her and her companion. Even Charity Dawkins, who had been allowed to come by special permission, stared. Lily Flowers looked stormy, and her sister pouted, while Harriet Hadley flirted with a reluctant Earl Castleton. Even the dowager duchess was eyeing them with disquiet, and Celia wondered why that should be so.

But as they bowled down the drive and the others were lost from sight behind them, Celia forgot them in a moment. And when they reached the road west, and the team settled into a mile-eating canter, she laughed her delight out loud. It was just as she had imagined, she told herself as she hung on to her bonnet. The beautiful team, the handsome man, the shiny phaeton—ah, romance, indeed! No wonder the others had stared. They were jealous.

A sudden, unpleasant thought occurred to her then, and she frowned.

"Now what are you thinking, Miss Anders?" the viscount asked, glancing sideways for a moment and seeing that frown. "A moment ago you were laughing, but now you glare. What is the reason?"

Celia refused to be drawn, and she shook her head and pretended she could not remember. Then, to distract him, she asked about the village they were approaching.

She did not hear a word he said, for she was examining the suspicion she had had that perhaps William Welburn had chosen to drive her to Bath as a sort of protection from the younger ladies of the party. Perhaps he had decided that neither of the Flowers twins would do, nor Miss Hadley, either. But by asking her, who was so much older, and so long the spinster, he could keep them at bay. As logical as this explanation was, it did nothing to elevate Celia's spirits. Still, she admonished herself, to be downcast was ridiculous. At her age she was not expecting romance, heavens, of course not. But she intended to take full advantage of what he offered and enjoy it to the hilt.

"How smoothly the team goes," she remarked. "They are so beautiful, too."

"They should be. They cost me a fortune," he told her. "Not that that is to be regarded. There are those who say nothing is more important than a man's horseflesh, but I have never held with anything so ridiculous. Men who believe that tend to think the clothes they wear and the splendor of their cravats to be next in importance in life. I don't hold with that idiocy, either."

"I am glad to hear you say so, sir. It reinforces

my original impression that you are a sensible man. Well, most of the time."

He smiled down at her, and Celia was glad she had worn the leaf green carriage dress and the stunning bonnet after all.

"I shall not ask you to explain that last remark, Miss Anders. You see, I intend to be on my best behavior all day and allow nothing you say or do to provoke me."

"I wonder if I could," Celia mused as if to herself. "It might be amusing to try. And surely there must be *something* that would upset you. Perhaps even make you testy, sir?"

The tiger's stifled cough reminded her they were not alone, and she flushed a little to Drummond's obvious amusement.

When they reached Bath, their pace was by necessity slowed. The town had been built at the base of some steep hills, and the streets were crowded, not only with carriages and carts, but with the sedan chairs used by the invalid and elderly residents. The viscount drove to York House. It was the finest inn, and the dowager had reserved private rooms for her party.

Turning the phaeton and pair over to his tiger's careful care, Drummond took Celia's arm.

"What would you like to see first, Miss Anders?" he asked. "The Abbey? The Pump Room? The Baths?"

"I shall allow you to choose, sir, and be my guide. What a delightful city this is."

"If you enjoy peace and quiet. Bath has fallen from fashion now, and is inhabited mainly by the old and infirm. Still, with the Avon winding through it, and the excellent architecture, it's a pleasant place. We must be sure to go up to the

Royal Crescent later, and on to Lansdowne Place. The view over the city from there is outstanding."

Celia was properly awed by the Abbey, and stunned by the Roman Baths. Above them, the elegant Pump Room intrigued her, and she was happy to take a seat and listen to the musicians playing on the balcony while the viscount went to get her a glass of the waters.

She made a face when she sniffed it, knowing now why he had not provided himself with a glass, too. Drummond told her to drink it right down, for it was supposed to be good for you. Celia wrinkled her nose as she obeyed. She had no intention of asking for seconds.

By the time they left the Pump Room, the rest of the party had arrived. Most of the gentlemen went to one of the libraries, to Meyler's or Duffield's, while some of the ladies set out to explore the excellent shops. Mrs. Dawkins took Charity away to sight-see, while her aunt and the dowager repaired to York House for a quiet chat.

Thinking that perhaps Drummond would prefer to spend some time with the gentlemen, Celia suggested he join them. She was told nothing was further from his mind, as he tucked her hand in his arm. The two of them walked toward Gay Street. It was quite a climb to the Circus and the Royal Crescent, but well worth the effort. And the view from Lansdowne Place was everything the viscount had promised.

After a leisurely repast at the inn, everyone dispersed again. Celia was beginning to feel a little uneasy at the length of time she had spent with the viscount, and was quick to suggest David Powers and Harriet Hadley join them as they set off to explore the parks and gardens. Besides, she had sensed the duchess was not best pleased with her godson's companion, and even kind Lady Cassandra had pursed her lips and frowned a little. Celia wondered why. And why had the Dawkins child given her a sly grin, so quickly gone Celia was not sure she hadn't imagined it.

But when the time came to return to the castle, and she suggested someone else be honored for the return trip, Drummond would have none of it.

"If you remember, Miss Anders, I asked you. You would not be so unkind as to leave me in midstream, now, would you? Come, the phaeton is ready. Let's be off."

Celia was not a bit reluctant to smile and agree. She had had a wonderful day. Drummond had been more than agreeable and pleasant, he had been an attentive host, treating her to the most distinguished civility. Under his attentions, she had bloomed, loving every minute. It would have been hard to give up the remainder of her treat, for that is how she had come to see this day—a glorious gift set down in the middle of her generally humdrum life. That there would probably never be another one, she refused to contemplate.

Having thrown caution to the winds, the drive back seemed much too short to Celia. Even forced as they both were by the tiger's silent presence to mind their tongues, she and William Welburn had a lively discussion on a number of subjects.

Celia was surprised at the knowledge and depth he displayed, and she wondered if there was any subject she could introduce that would find him lacking in understanding. And to think she had considered him little better than a fashionable man-about-town. How embarrassing it was, remembering that.

Of course they reached the castle well before the others, and they were alone when Drummond came to lift her down from the phaeton. Did his hands linger for a moment on her waist? she wondered, schooling her face to nonchalance. Was it her imagination that he was slow to set her on her feet? His dark eyes stared down into hers, and she felt her breathing quicken. Stop it, Celia, she commanded herself. Think of something—anything!—to say. But before she could stammer out her thanks for the lovely day and his especial escort, he leaned closer and, taking her hands in his, said, "I have been the true gentleman today, have I not, Miss Anders? Behaved myself impeccably? What a shame such behavior cannot last. You see, I have been meaning to ask you whether you enjoyed reading Duke Wentworth's old stud book? I thought it an unusual choice for one who does not even ride. But then, you have shown me today how broad your interests are."

Indignant, Celia stiffened. But before she could speak, he went on smoothly. "You must admit it was a strange choice for a lady. Do tell me why you selected it. If you can, that is."

Celia pulled her hands free of his and curtsied. "I could, of course, but I think I will not. To be quite blunt about it, my reading habits are none of your concern. Give you good afternoon, sir."

As she hurried up the steps, he called after her, "That was unworthy of you, Miss Anders. I expected much better."

Celia pretended she had not heard him, nor his little chuckle, and she gave the porter a heartfelt smile when he admitted her to the castle so promptly.

She remained secluded in her room until the final dinner bell that evening. She told herself she was not being a coward; she really needed to have a bath and wash her hair. And that evening, when the viscount divided his time between the dowager and Lady Cassandra, she told herself how glad she was, knowing full well she was lying in both instances.

A long time later Celia Anders tried to remember when things began to change for her. Had it been that day they had all spent in Bath? Or was it later she had started to feel uncomfortable? she asked herself. She remembered that when she had gone down to breakfast, she had waved a footman away when he hurried forward to open the breakfast room door for her because she had heard something she did not care to share with even a servant.

Lady Flowers had been speaking, and her words had effectively stayed Celia in her tracks. "Well, I have always said that even though you dress mutton like lamb, when all is said and done, you'll still end up with mutton. Remember that, girls."

Celia was tempted to hurry back to her room, but she sensed the footman was staring at her, and she pretended to search for something in her work bag before she took a deep breath and nodded to him.

The entire Flowers family was at the table, and with her nerves on edge, Celia found their stares, their sudden silence, disconcerting. She was delighted when Lady Cassandra and Bart Whitaker came in shortly thereafter.

The morning was spent rehearsing the play, so it could not have been then. But sometime during that day Celia came to feel the cynosure of every female eye. But surely, she told herself, this is ridiculous! I must be imagining things, for just going to Bath with Viscount Drummond could not have produced so universal a distaste of me. Or am I being too sensitive? She remembered her uncle Dudley had often told her in her early teens that she must not suppose people were staring at her and discussing her every move to her detriment, for such was not the case. And she was not a young girl now, in agonies over her appearance and behavior. She was twenty-nine years old.

She wished she were closer to the dowager. She knew Dolly Farrington, for all her heedless gaiety, was a kind woman, and an astute one. But their one meeting in London, and being invited to the castle, did not constitute the kind of friendship that allowed one to confide one's troubles.

For some reason, the viscount's handsome face came to mind, and she shook her head. What was she thinking? she scolded herself. Tell Drummond that she was sure people were talking about her? Snubbing her as Miss Hadley had done that morning by ducking back into her room when Celia passed by, to avoid joining her? He would be sure to tell her she was only the latest victim of their resident gossip and demand to know what was being said about her. And he would laugh. She could almost hear him.

Still, when she came upon him suddenly late one afternoon in the gardens where she had fled to be alone and think, she almost blurted out her troubles with her first breath.

"Come out to inspect the gardens, Miss Anders?" he asked as he offered his arm. "Can't say I find much to admire here myself, but there's no accounting for tastes."

He stared down at a patch of dead vegetation, and shrugged. "But perhaps a garden full of blooms and scents is too overpowering for you?"

"No, it's not," Celia said briskly. As they turned to stroll up the slight rise to the castle, she kept her eyes firmly away from all those windows staring down at them. Anyone might be standing at one of them, she reminded herself, wondering what she and the viscount had been doing together, but she would not give anyone the satisfaction of seeing her look up anxiously.

Drummond paused in full view of the windows and turned her toward him. "I have not seen much of you these past few days," he said easily, his dark eyes searching her face. "You seem to have been avoiding the company. Is everything all right?"

Celia stifled the urge she still felt to confide in him. "Why, everything is just fine," she made herself say as she smiled up at him. "Now perhaps you would let me go, sir? We are within sight of the castle, and anyone could be watching us and drawing all the wrong conclusions."

Instead of releasing her, his hands tightened. "And that would bother you, Miss Anders?" he asked, bending still nearer. "Surely you cannot care what a bunch of old biddies think of you, do you? I imagined you to be more intrepid.

"But if they are watching, let's really give them something to chew over at tea," he said as he drew her into his arms. When it came, his kiss was warm and intimate and slow, and his hands held her captive against his chest. Celia could feel his heart beating, smell the seductive scent of him. Conscious of everything about him, still she felt as if every inch of her were concentrated on their two pair of lips, his tender yet demanding, hers afraid but still yearning.

He did not end the embrace or let her go, and Celia stopped thinking of the people who might be watching and what evil might come of this mad taunting of society's rules. Suddenly, she did not care. Her lips opened under his and she sighed into his mouth. She admitted her surrender when her arms crept up around his neck and her hands lost themselves in his hair. His arms tightened and his hands caressed her back as his tongue invaded her mouth. She was startled only for a moment. How wonderful it felt, she thought dreamily as she tried to get closer to him still.

When he lifted his head at last, and cool afternoon air took the place of his lips on hers, she opened her eyes slowly, to stare up at him, dazed. To her surprise, he was frowning. But why would that be so? she wondered. Hadn't he enjoyed their kiss as much as she had? He had certainly appeared to.

Then reason returned, and she felt herself pale. Pulling away from him, she picked up her skirts and prepared to run.

"Wait!" he commanded, although he did not touch her again. She told herself she was glad of that, and knew she lied.

"I must speak with you, Miss Anders—no, *Celia*. I never meant, I mean, I did not intend to . . ."

Stung that he was regretting what she knew would be the most wonderful few minutes of her entire life, she backed away from him. "It is unnecessary to say any more, sir. Indeed, I pray you will not," she managed to stammer. "You—we—made a mistake. Best we forget it."

Before he could reply, she ran away from him, up the gentle slope to one of the side doors of the castle. She hoped she could reach her room without meeting anyone, for she was sure her emotions were written plain for anyone to see.

Luck was with her, and she closed her door to lean back against it, panting. Her hands moved to touch her burning cheeks, and when at last she went to her dressing table to remove her bonnet, she was shocked by her reflection. She looked not only wild but wanton, and most thoroughly kissed.

And for someone who was not at all romantic, never had been, and never intended to be, she was completely undone.

Below, in one of the smaller salons where he had sought refuge, much as Celia had, William Welburn was pouring himself a glass of Canary and wondering what on earth had come over him. He had not intended to kiss Miss Anders, not the first time it had happened, or today.

He sat down on one of Dolly's comfortable sofas and reviewed his behavior. It was true, the first time he had met Miss Anders on the bridle path he had kissed her almost in jest. He knew her age; surely she had engaged in some little lovemaking many times before this, and she would know the rules. There was no one else here at all suitable for a light flirtation, or even a discreet affair, if he could entice her to one. Those Flowers twins, besides setting his teeth on edge with their silly chatter, were intent on finding husbands, as was the much-maligned Miss Hadley. Any encouragement on his part in their direction would result in that long-dreaded march down the aisle and the mocking congratulations of his friends. But he was sure Celia Anders was not likely to expect that happy ending. Not at her age.

Still, he remembered how unpracticed her kiss had been, how he had been sure he was the first man to embrace her that way. He had been stunned, and more than a little troubled, and he had not attempted anything of the sort again.

Until today.

He had enjoyed their trip to Bath more than he had thought he would. Miss Anders was not only sensible, well read, and well opinioned, she had a sense of humor she was not always able to conceal.

And he had known how she had reveled in her delight that she was seated beside him in the phaeton. He had even known the moment she had stopped protesting when he insisted on spending the day with her, and with her alone. And he had known almost to the minute when she had ceased worrying about what others might think, to throw herself into the experience with abandon. He had been as sorry as he suspected she was when they arrived back at the castle and he had had to let her go.

Was that why he had twitted her about the duke's stud book, then? he wondered. Because he felt things were getting out of hand? For both of them?

Drummond frowned. His godmother had taken him to task that same day. She had sent him a note asking him to come to her boudoir before they had to change for dinner. He had gone, of course, to suffer the unpleasant experience of being chastised like a small, naughty boy.

"I have told you before, I will not have it, William," she had scolded, looking quite fierce even though she barely came up to his shoulder. "You will not—do you hear me?—*not* make a mockery of that poor young woman. No, indeed! She does not know your kind, and she is vulnerable in a way other women are not. And no, I have no intention of telling you any more about her situation. You will have to believe me when I tell you Celia Anders is not for you, not in any way. To form a connection with her can only lead to disaster. Leave her alone!

"Yes, I know how old you are, and I know I have no right to give you orders, or lecture you on your behavior. But I invited the girl here, and I am responsible for her. Her uncle has his head in a fog bank; he sees nothing. But I do, thank you very much, and I do not care for what I see. Behave yourself or I shall be very, very cross with you."

There had been a long pause before Drummond could control his temper and give her a reassuring reply. And true to his word, he had stayed away from Miss Anders, although he had regretted that. Compared to her, the other women here were insipid, but he could not remain with the gentlemen exclusively, lest he be thought rag-mannered. Now he wondered again what there was about Celia Anders that made her so ineligible, and, if she were, why his godmother had invited her. It was a mystery.

As he rose to pour another glass of wine, he suddenly remembered why he had kissed her that afternoon. It had been an urge impossible to deny, and it had had nothing whatsoever to do with gossiping old ladies. No, it had happened because she had looked so quiet and grave, even unhappy, that he had been moved to take her in his arms.

Drummond set the decanter down and replaced the stopper slowly as he recalled how her lips had felt under his, how warm and trusting, and finally giving. And how she had felt in his arms, her slim height a perfect match for him, the soft curves of her breasts and hips teasing his senses.

And now he remembered how she had looked when he let her go at last. Her pink lips had quivered ever so slightly, and her face had been full of delicate color. But it had been her hazel eyes that had stunned him into silence. Large and glowing, they had looked at him in complete delight. And with complete trust as well. He groaned. Dear God, what had he done?

Ten

THINGS SEEMED A little better to Celia, and she began to think that perhaps the other ladies at the house party had grown tired of gossiping about her. As well they should, she thought as she sat in the largest drawing room with them, doing some desultory stitchery so she could keep her eyes cast down. Viscount Drummond, although civil, was so distant, no one could suspect a possible relationship. His defection had caused her many a sleepless hour, for although he still spoke to her on occasion, even asked her to dance and join his team for charades, he treated her so formally you would think they had just been introduced. Celia sighed, then looked up hastily, wondering if Lady Powers had heard her from her seat across the way.

Louisa Powers had other things on her mind that afternoon. She was still in a constant state of worry lest her son should somehow discover her relationship with Lord Manchester. It was just the sort of thing some men would take great delight in relating to others, she thought gloomily as she snipped a loose scarlet thread. Indeed, she had long suspected men were worse gossips than women, although they would be sure to deny any such thing. Take that awful Mr. Grey, for example. It would be just like him to tell David, hoping to make him as miserable as he appeared to be himself. She glanced up to where his wife was bent over her horrid altar cloth and told herself she supposed she could not blame the man. Married to that impossible specimen of womanhood would be enough to turn anyone sour. She wondered that the dowager had asked them, until she remembered they were related to the present duke's bride.

Her gaze went to the bracket clock on the mantel. David had asked her to join him for a stroll at two, and she did not want to be late. Seeing the time, she folded her needlepoint carefully and put it away before she rose and excused herself.

It was blustery that April day when the two of them left the castle and headed down the drive. How good it was to be alone with him, Lady Powers thought. And it wouldn't be much longer before they were both back in London. How she missed her dear grandchildren!

As they turned off on a side path, she hugged his arm in delight. He was her only son and very precious to her. There was no one she loved more, not even Alastair, and heaven knew how much she loved him.

"Mother, there is something we must discuss," David said. Louisa Powers felt a small frisson of unease.

"I received a note this morning," he went on, and she made herself concentrate. "It was not signed, nor did I recognize the handwriting. It seemed disguised to me, almost primitive. But I shall show it to you, and you shall be the judge."

He stopped then and drew a piece of paper from his coat. Reluctantly, his mother took it from him and opened it slowly. It was just as she had feared. The writer asked if David knew his mother was in love with a man who wasn't her husband, and had been for years. It even named Alastair, to Lady Powers's horror, and it was so sly, so salacious somehow, her eyes filled with tears and she could not restrain a sob.

At once David's arms came around her in support. "Don't cry, Mother," he said. "There is no need to be upset."

"But—but I have always been so careful to keep it from you," she wailed softly. "I never meant to hurt you, son, never! It is just that Alastair and I have loved each other forever. And now, because of someone's spite, all your trust in me, and your love, has been lost."

"No such thing," he told her briskly as he handed her his handkerchief. "Here now, dry your eyes. Besides, I have known of your love for Lord Manchester since I was twelve."

"You have?" his mother asked, her eyes wide. "But—but ..."

"It has never changed my feeling for you, Mother," he said, smiling to reassure her. "I think Lord Manchester a fine man. And knowing my father as I do, I cannot fault you for leaving him. But why didn't the two of you consider divorce?"

"Oh, no," Lady Powers said in a stronger voice. "I could never do such a thing, for it would reflect on you and haunt your children's lives. Alastair understands. He is willing to wait for me."

She blushed a little as her son chuckled. "What a very patient man he is, to be sure," he remarked. "But come, my dear, are you more at ease now? For since I do know, whoever sent this note cannot hurt you anymore. I must admit I do wonder who it could be, though. Don't you?"

Her heart was so much lighter, Louisa Powers felt she had lost a stone of weight, and several years as well as they set off again. It did not even matter who had made the mischief. Not now. But to think David had known of her infidelity for such a long time! To think it did not matter to him, that he loved her still! She was, she told herself, a very fortunate woman in spite of everything that had happened to her in her sad and eventful life.

The play was coming along well now. Sometimes whole scenes passed without Celia having to cue. The twins had finally conquered their giggles as they grew more accustomed to their part, and even Miss Hadley seemed able to forget she was called a thief here, when she was deep in her role. Earl Castleton had the most trouble with Charles Danforth. The poet had abandoned his writing for the duration of rehearsals, but he seemed bent on applying his talent to expanding his part.

He was wont to go off on wild tangents, striding about the newly erected stage and throwing his hands out as he spoke his lines, and any additional ones that occurred to him, until he was called to order by the director.

Poor Miss Hadley bore the brunt of his digressions, for, as the heroine, most of her scenes were played with him. Celia could not help chuckling when he finally stopped carrying on and Miss Hadley spoke the lines written that had now, because of his histrionics, no meaning at all. And she could not help thinking Viscount Drummond must share her amusement until she remembered his sudden coolness toward her.

"You do see, Danforth, how difficult it is for the others when you go off on your own like that, do you not?" the earl demanded one morning when Mr. Danforth was even wordier than usual. "If you keep adding to your speech, poor Miss Hadley will be all at sea trying to follow you. Just now, for example, you added an entire new speech, ending, 'I shall stand firm, clinging to my principles, and I shall gladly die to defend them.'

"That's all very well, old chap, but Miss Hadley's next line was, 'Dear, dear. I fear it will rain this afternoon so we must cancel the picnic.' Where's the sense of that?"

Danforth had looked a little disgusted even as he had been forced to admit it didn't make any.

The men in the play dealt with him themselves. Mr. Grey just snarled at him, and Viscount Drummond did not hesitate to interrupt whenever the poet began to emote. But then, he was the villain, so that was unremarkable. Bart Whitaker, as the hero's friend, had much the more difficult role, which he carried off with careless aplomb.

Several people wandered in and out during rehearsals, as well as those servants engaged in costume and scenery making. And Charity Dawkins was always there. She sat alone, very quietly, in the back of the room, and few people were even aware of her.

Celia wondered why the little girl found the play so interesting, especially after hearing a tricky scene rehearsed four times in a row. She must be lonesome indeed, poor child, she thought one morning when they were finishing, and Charity slipped from the room. No doubt she will be glad to leave here and get to London. I suppose I should ask Mrs. Dawkins to bring her to visit there one day, but somehow, I cannot bring myself to do so. She is so very strange. So quiet. It is unnatural.

She saw Drummond coming down the steps from the stage, and she turned away in haste. Better to pretend she did not see him, she told herself as she gathered up her copy of the play. But the viscount was in a deep discussion with Earl Castleton about the best way to get the effect of a shot offstage without actually firing a pistol, and the two men passed her without a word. This depressed Celia so much that she lost her appetite completely, and instead of following the others in to nuncheon, she went slowly up to her room. Behind her, alone now, Viscount Drummond watched her go, and his mouth tightened before he turned abruptly toward the library.

That evening after dinner and the gentlemen's customary glasses of port, the dowager called everyone to order in the drawing room. "I hope you will recall our game of hide-and-seek," she said with a smile as she beckoned to a footman holding a glass bowl that contained a number of folded slips of paper. "The time has come to choose our fox, if I may be permitted to compare our game to the hunt?

"I have made out slips, each with one name on it, and now it is time to draw that name. I warn you, you cannot refuse the honor if you are chosen. Are we all agreed on that?"

Everyone nodded or clapped, although with varying degrees of enthusiasm. Celia noted Mr. Grey looked disgusted, Lady Cassandra most reluctant, and the twins ready to giggle if either of them should be chosen. Why, even Miss Hadley was sitting forward in her chair in anticipation.

"William, my dear, you're closest," Dolly Farrington said. "Please take out one slip so we may know our fox."

As he began to obey, she added, "Stir them up well now, and close your eyes. This must be fair."

Drummond obeyed, although to Celia he looked bored by the whole thing. Maybe he felt, as she was sure most of the gentlemen did, that this childhood game was not only ridiculous but undignified for adults to indulge in. But perhaps they had all of them been at the castle too long, and it was time to go home?

At last Drummond handed a single slip of paper to the dowager and moved away as she opened it. At once her silvery laugh rang out, and shaking her head, she said, "My dears, you will never guess. Drummond has drawn his own name! Now, isn't that a famous joke?"

Celia watched the viscount's face grow still as everyone began to speak all at once. He stared at his godmother, but she did not notice, for she was handing the bowl back to the footman, who bowed and carried it away. But what on earth was Drummond thinking? Celia wondered before she turned her back on him to ask Mr. Whitaker where he thought the viscount would hide.

"I've no idea, ma'am," that gentleman said. "There are any number of choices in the old wing, of course. And knowing Drummond, he'll lead us a merry chase. I say, Your Grace," he added, raising his voice slightly, "are the searchers to be given a time limit? It would be fairer to our fox that way."

"What a good idea, sir," she exclaimed. "Yes, I agree that would be wise. And shall we say tomorrow afternoon at two for the game? It is supposed to rain then."

"Not tomorrow, rain or not," the viscount said firmly. It grew quiet as he added, "I must have some time to prepare. This is one fox who intends to confound the hounds."

The guests scoffed, for most of them were determined to be the winner themselves. The prize was a rare framed pen and ink drawing of a young girl in a garden done by the American artist John Copley early in his career, and everyone coveted it.

"I'll let you know when I'm ready," Drummond said.

"Oh, very well, although I think you are mean to make us wait," his godmother said lightly. "Now, what amount of time does everyone think would be fair? There are some twenty rooms and several corridors and stairways in the old wing, as well as the main hall and armory. I hereby declare the lower levels with their dungeons and such not part of the hunt. They are a dark, dusty rabbit warren. Too difficult."

"I wonder if that is fair?" Drummond mused. "They sound like the perfect place to hide."

"Except everyone would hurry down there, to stumble over each other first thing," Duke Ainsworth remarked. "Her Grace is right. Let's omit them."

Drummond nodded. "Shall we say a thirty-minute time limit?" he asked, looking around. "Surely twenty rooms can be searched by then, especially by so many people."

Several guests disagreed, and after a further discussion, forty-five minutes was agreed to.

But Celia had to wonder at the viscount's intentness now. It was almost as if, having been chosen, he was determined to win at any cost. And his making the others wait until he had found the perfect hiding place showed his determination. It was only a child's game, after all. Why would he care so much?

She mentioned this to Mr. Whitaker and Duke Ainsworth as the others dispersed, some to play cards, others to listen to an impromptu concert of duets sung by the twins.

Bart laughed a little. "William Welburn hates to lose. At anything. He may not have wanted to have anything to do with this scheme of Her Grace's, but having been chosen, he will do everything he can to win. I have never known a fiercer competitor. You

119

remember, Duke, that race we had to Richmond last spring? Drummond went so far as to purchase a new team and train it, and he won handily. Not many men would go to all that trouble."

Celia rose as the dowager smiled and beckoned to her. As she moved away, Whitaker murmured to his friend, "I'd give a great deal to inspect that bowl Her Grace had prepared for the drawing, wouldn't you?"

Ainsworth stared at him, and a tiny smile curved the corners of his mouth. "You don't really think she did that, do you, Bart?" he asked.

"I wouldn't put it past her. It would be just like Dolly Farrington to get the fox she wanted by putting Drummond's name on all the slips. Only consider how deadly the game would have been if Grey's name had been chosen, or Lady Cassandra's. But we'll never find out now if she manipulated the outcome. You saw how quick she was to have the footman remove the bowl. I'd wager anything those slips are nothing but ashes now."

The viscount was late to rehearsal the next morning, and he disappeared to the old wing right after it, setting his valet to guard the door that led to it. It was late afternoon before he beckoned Mr. Petson to join him inside.

If anyone had been interested, he would have seen the satisfied smiles both men sported when they left the wing. The next morning, Mr. Petson set out very early for Bath. He did not return until afternoon, and when he entered the castle he had a number of parcels with him which he refused to entrust to anyone else.

But no one, with the exception of Charity Dawkins, paid any attention to the viscount or his valet, and Charity learned nothing, for Mr. Petson was extremely closemouthed, which was one of the reasons he had been employed in the first place. She entered his name in her notebook, scowling as she did so.

That evening, the viscount announced that the game could take place the following afternoon, but at three, not two. He also stipulated that anyone who was caught investigating the old wing before that time would forfeit his chance of playing.

"How very mysterious you are, William, and how severe," the dowager teased. "Giving orders left and right! I do believe you intend to best everyone, don't you?"

"I shall be most surprised if I am found, ma'am. I say no more than that."

The others scoffed. With the game of hide-and-seek to look forward to, they spent a lively evening, dancing and discussing just how they intended to prove the arrogant Viscount Drummond wrong.

Eleven

DRUMMOND DISAPPEARED INTO the old wing immediately after the morning's play rehearsals ended. He was speeded on his way by the jeers of the others, all of whom warned him he would be discovered in the shortest time. He ignored them, although his gaze went fleetingly to where Celia was bent over her copy of the play. He was disappointed. He would have liked her to smile at him and encourage him. Then he sneered at himself. Whatever was the matter with him, he wondered, that he put so much store in one not-very-young, not-very-beautiful woman's smile?

At the door that led to the old wing, he was met by his valet. Petson had a large case with him, and he bowed as he ushered the viscount inside and closed the door behind them.

"Anyone try to get in here this morning?" Drummond asked as he strode down a corridor that led to the great hall.

"Only that Dawkins child, sir. I've never seen a little one as determined as that. Had to speak harshly to her, I did, before she'd give up and go away."

He did not add that the little girl had threatened to tell her mother on him, nor how she had glowered. He was sure he must have caught a chill then, for he had begun to shiver.

Strange that, he mused now. He was not a man

unnerved by the threats of children. At least he hadn't been till then.

Petson forgot Charity Dawkins when the viscount beckoned him into one of the chambers off the great hall. He hurried forward and began to unpack his case, laying a large sheet carefully on the floor first.

An hour later they were surprised by that persistent young miss. She had sneaked into the wing to look around, inquisitive as always. The viscount treated her to a blistering setdown and ordered Petson to hand her over to the butler's care. Bogle was told that on no account was Miss Dawkins to be allowed to speak to any of the guests, including her mother. She was to be kept sequestered in the housekeeper's room until exactly three forty-five, with a sturdy footman set to guard her.

At three, when the guests assembled before the door that led to the oldest wing, Miss Dawkins was one of the few who was not among them. Even the Greys had condescended to join the fun, more from curiosity than anything else. Only Celia's uncle Dudley and his crony, Reginald Stark, were missing. The dowager declared she would not play either, just before she gave the signal to begin.

"It would not be right, for I might win my own prize," she told them. As the clock began to strike the hour, she waved her hands. "Off with you," she cried. "May the best hunter win!"

The Flowers twins were the fleetest and they rushed forward, beating Miss Hadley to the door handily. The others streamed in behind them, Bart Whitaker and Duke Ainsworth bringing up the rear. These gentlemen strolled down the corridor that led to the great hall, inspecting the rooms that lined it on either side, but finding nothing.

"I didn't expect we would," Bart said at last. "Although it might have been a good ploy for Drummond to have hidden in the first one, trusting we would rush by, then slipping out of the wing after we were all inside."

"Unethical, old man. Not fair at all," Ainsworth protested.

"Oh, I'm sure he would have come back, forty minutes from now or so. Remember his determination not to be found. And no one said he couldn't move around, even leave the wing."

They were both silent when they entered the great hall and looked around. They could hear the voices of the other players as they ran from room to room above them. Only the elderly Mr. Grey remained there, trailed by his wife as he checked behind every tapestry and peered into the visors of the suits of armor along the walls.

The hall rose two stories to huge rafters and cross beams. Ainsworth pointed up at them, brows raised. But peer as they might into the gloom, they could discern no trace of William Welburn stretched out there on top of one. The hall was almost a vast, empty space. Only those suits of armor and the occasional chair stood against walls that were covered by the shields, battle-axes, and lances of an earlier day. There were also a few pieces of marble statuary scattered about on pedestals. It was not an inviting room in spite of the blaze in the enormous fireplace that fought valiantly to dispel the chill.

Somewhere above them a door slammed, and they moved toward the staircase that led upward from the hall. Behind them, Mr. Grey continued his meticulous search while his wife tried to look interested.

Celia Anders had begun her own search for the viscount almost reluctantly, for she was not at all sure she wanted to be the one who found him, after the way he had been acting. But she had become caught up in the excitement of the chase, and was soon rushing from one room to another as eagerly as anyone else. Only when she found herself peeking into a chest at the foot of one of the beds did she scold herself for being so silly. The chest was much too small to contain the tall, wide-shouldered viscount. Neither could he be under the beds, for they were built low to the ground, so she might just as well stop getting down on her hands and knees to look, and doing nothing but get dust on her gown.

She had gone through every room, some of them more than once, long before the allotted time was up, and now she made her way back to the great hall. It was deserted and she stared up into the dimness above her, wondering, as Duke Ainsworth had, if the viscount could have somehow reached by ladder or by rope those massive cross beams she could barely see. For a while she continued to stare up at them, for she had the most uneasy feeling she was not alone. Suddenly she spun around, almost expecting to see someone creeping up on her, the feeling was so strong. Then she scoffed at herself even though she had to rub her arms to get rid of the goose bumps there. Sighing, she sat down on one of the leather chairs set against the wall and admitted defeat.

A few minutes later, the dowager duchess entered the hall directly across from her. Celia rose and curtsied.

"Have you given up, Miss Anders?" that lady asked gaily. "But never mind. It is time for me to call the others back, for the game is over."

"I confess I did give up," Celia admitted. "The viscount is not to be found anywhere. I don't believe anyone else has found him, either, for surely I would have heard the commotion. How clever he has been! It is as if he vanished into thin air."

"Yes, it is famous," the dowager said as she clapped her hands. "I knew he would lead you all a merry chase, which is why I made sure he would be our fox."

She saw Celia's puzzled look, and said in a stage whisper, "I put his name on *all* the slips in that bowl. Drummond is not the only clever one here!"

She sounded so proud of herself, Celia had to chuckle. But still, she felt uneasy again.

As she looked around, the dowager rang a large bell she carried, holding it high as she turned slowly. The sound echoed off the stone walls. "Time is up, yes, indeed, the game is over," she called. "You must all return to the great hall now."

By ones and twos, the guests straggled back, complaining of the viscount's cleverness.

"I'm sure he must have cheated somehow," Lily Flowers said, pouting. "Why, we have looked everywhere and—"

"He was nowhere to be found," Rose finished.

"I think so myself," Mr. Grey said, for once agreeable. "In fact, I'm sure he is not in this part of the castle at all. And probably never was. Hmmph!"

Celia saw Charity Dawkins enter the room then and begin to sidle around it. She was wondering why, when her attention was caught by a strange couple dressed in traveling clothes who had just entered the hall. They both looked around as if amazed.

"Well, 'pon my soul," the gentleman said as he removed his top hat and gloves. "What on earth is going on here, Mother?"

"Kendall?" Her Grace asked, leaning forward to

126

peer at him as if she could not believe her eyes. "What are *you* doing here?"

"This *is* my castle, is it not?" the man Celia knew now for the duke replied. In spite of his teasing words, he did not seem amused, and he looked around slowly at all the people gathered in the great hall. How different he was from his mother, Celia thought. No one would ever suspect them of being related, for where the dowager was tiny and slight, her son was almost corpulent, and he had an air of pompous dignity Dolly Farrington would have scorned to adopt.

"Well, of course it is, my dear. Don't be absurd," the dowager duchess said. Then she added with a smile, "Forgive me for not greeting you sooner, Eunice. I forgot in the shock of your appearance, for I did not expect you until May. I mean, one rarely rushes home early from a honeymoon. At least I didn't."

Embarrassed, the new duchess sported two patches of bright red on her pale cheeks as the duke said, "Do mind your tongue, Mother! I suppose we can come home when we want to. Besides, neither the duchess nor I cared for the Continent or traveling. And the food was atrocious.

"But you have not answered my question," he added, a querulous note in his voice. "Why are all these people here in the old wing? It is never used anymore."

Before his mother could explain, a deep voice said, "We were having a game of hide-and-seek, sir, and I do believe I have just won it."

Everyone turned toward that voice and stared as Viscount Drummond, covered in some sort of grayish white powder and paint, and wearing only an abbreviated toga and sandals of the same color,

127

climbed down from one of the pedestals where he had been posing.

As he stretched his sore muscles, the twins shrieked in fright, and Mrs. Grey, who had been closest to the pedestal, slid quietly to the floor in a faint. Concerned, Lord Manchester put his arm around Lady Powers in support, and a horrified Lady Cassandra covered her face with her handkerchief. Even the new bride leaned against her husband and moaned. Celia did not know whether to exclaim or laugh at Drummond. His disguise had been excellent, for as long as he remained motionless, no one would have suspected he was not just another marble statue. And how clever he had been to hide right out in the open, where no one would expect to find him! Of course, she admitted, being in a dim corner of the hall had certainly helped. And now she knew why she had had the uneasy feeling she had not been alone here.

The viscount's valet came forward then, carrying a cloak. Before he put it over his master's broad shoulders, Celia, and everyone else, had a very good look at the viscount's almost naked physique. Well-muscled and without an ounce of fat, it was certainly attention-getting, she thought, noticing how everyone was staring still, especially Miss Hadley and the twins. Then she had to cover her mouth with her hand lest she chuckle, for both twins had their mouths identically agape.

"Drummond? Can that be you, man?" the duke asked in the sudden silence. His eyes were popping as he patted his wife's back with a distracted hand. "I can't believe my eyes."

"You should," the viscount replied. As he donned the cloak Mr. Petson was holding, puffs of white powder swirled in the air, and he coughed a little. "This may have been an excellent ruse, but I think

I must brave the outdoors to beat most of the powder away before I am fit for company."

Now that he was decently covered, Lady Cassandra recovered her poise and sent him a burning, accusing stare. Lady Powers knelt beside the still-unconscious Mrs. Grey to wave a vinaigrette under her nose.

"I do beg the ladies' pardon for startling them," Drummond said. "My hand was forced, you see." He stared then at Charity Dawkins, who was standing beside her mother, looking grim.

"And that is all you have to say?" the duke demanded, his face scarlet. "Here I arrive home with my duchess after a lengthy, tiring journey, looking forward to some peace and tranquillity, to discover my seat invaded by a group of people playing a children's game. And one of them almost naked at that! You should be ashamed of yourself, sir! I must say I find your attitude and moral laxity disgusting. Beg the ladies' pardon, indeed! I should think that is the least you should do!"

"Are you waiting for me to beg your pardon, too, Your Grace?" Drummond drawled. "I had no idea you were so, er, nice."

"I am known to have the understanding of sensible men," His Grace retorted. "Besides, I still don't know what you and everyone else is doing here at the castle."

"And I have to wonder what the duke and his new bride will make of the dowager's nude statues in the woods, don't you, Duke?" Bartholomew Whitaker murmured to his friend. Mr. Ainsworth was seized by an attack of coughing and could not reply.

"Oh, of all the ridiculous things," Dolly Farrington exclaimed. "You sound positively bird-witted, Kendall. And very ungracious, too, I might add.

Surely it is obvious I am giving a house party. I can't understand why that is not evident to you. And if you hadn't come home so unexpectedly, you would never have learned of it. Besides, you know most of these people as well as I do, yet still you act as if I had filled the place with tinkers and Gypsies. And you, Eunice, don't you see your relatives, the Greys, are also here?"

As if the mention of her name had restored her to consciousness, Mrs. Grey moaned then and everyone's attention turned to her as she struggled to sit up. Celia heard the viscount murmur from his place beside her, "I did think very hard, trying to let you know I was here, Miss Anders, so you would win the prize. Didn't you have any suspicion of it?"

"Why—why, yes. But I never suspected the statues. My congratulations. You fooled us all finely. But wasn't it difficult to remain motionless for such a length of time?"

"Not really. I had to hold still only when someone was in the hall. Of course, I did think Mr. Grey would find me out. He spent almost fifteen minutes here. In fact, I was sure he would never leave."

"We must hope his wife has taken no permanent harm," Celia said. She sounded reproving.

The viscount only grinned at her, and her lips started to quiver in spite of her good intentions.

"What amuses you?" he demanded.

"You do. It seems so funny to be talking to a marble man with white hair. Why, you are white all over."

"Not quite," he drawled, cocking a wicked brow at her.

Celia ordered herself not to blush.

"Your attention, please," the dowager called, and the excited, whispered conversations that everyone had been indulging in ceased.

"It is time to award the prize to the winner of our little adventure. Bogle?"

The butler came forward, carrying the framed drawing on a silver tray.

Holding it up, the dowager said, "I am sure we are all agreed that Drummond has been much too clever for us and has certainly won the game. Here you are, dear, sly fox."

As she moved toward him, drawing in hand, a cool, well-bred although expressionless voice remarked, "But I see it is well we returned when we did, my love. No doubt it is just like your dear mama to be so generous, but it will not do, no, not at all."

The new Duchess Wentworth turned to the dowager then and added, "Forgive me for pointing it out to you, dear ma'am, but you must not be giving away what belongs to the duke without his permission. But perhaps you forgot he is the owner of the castle and everything in it? Of course! You were not thinking clearly. Most understandable at your age."

Dolly Farrington appeared stunned for a moment, then she gave her silvery laugh, completely amused. Her new daughter-in-law's brows rose in amazement.

"You quite mistake the matter, Eunice," she said, smiling. "I would never dispose of any of my son's inheritance. This drawing, however, never belonged to him. It was given to me by his father while we were on our, er, long, *extended* honeymoon.

"Now that I see how much you covet it, I am so sorry I chose it as the prize. I would have been happy for you to have it. After my demise, of course. But unfortunately, it is now Viscount Drummond's.

"And I should point out, Eunice, there are a great many of my personal possessions in the castle. How

131

unfortunate you thought Kendall the owner of everything. I do hope it will not completely overset you when I take them with me to the dower house."

The dowager smiled at her quietly seething daughter-in-law before she handed the drawing to her godson, reaching up to kiss him as she did so. Wisdom arrived before her lips touched his face, and she backed away, shaking her head. "I shall kiss you later, sir, after you have dispensed with your disguise."

"And I shall have a few things to say to you at that time, Your Grace," he replied, staring hard at her.

She laughed again before she beckoned to the others. "Come, let us adjourn to a warmer part of the castle. And, Kendall, Eunice, I am so eager to hear all your news. Besides, you must be longing for a pot of good English tea. Come along, all of you!"

Relieved, the houseguests moved rapidly toward the door to the hall, happy to escape any more dialogue between the former and present duchess. If anyone had been taking wagers on who would win the next encounter between them, they would, to a man, have put their money on Dolly Farrington. But that did not mean they wanted to be an audience to it. Even Mrs. Grey hurried out, for although she was as eager as ever for new gossip, she did not like the way her niece was glaring at her new mama, her pale face blotched with red again. And she had suddenly remembered Eunice's ungovernable temper as a child.

Among the last to leave were Drusilla Dawkins and her daughter. Mrs. Dawkins walked beside Harriet Hadley, tossing her head as she said, "Nothing is at all fair here! By all rights the Copley drawing should have gone to my clever little Charity. She discovered what the viscount was up to early this afternoon when he was donning his powder and paint. And do you know what that horrid man had the audacity to do, ma'am?"

Miss Hadley confessed her ignorance, and Mrs. Dawkins rushed on. "He actually had Charity imprisoned in the housekeeper's room till just a few minutes ago so she could not claim the prize. And he dared to say if she screamed for help, he would have her gagged. Imagine! Threatening a little girl! The brute!"

"But your daughter was not playing the game with us, ma'am," Miss Hadley ventured to point out. "How could she have won? And it would not have been at all fair to the rest of us if she had told you alone about the viscount's scheme, now, would it?"

Mrs. Dawkins sniffed in derision. It was obvious she thought her darling daughter could do no wrong, and no argument, no matter how well reasoned, could make her change her mind.

Charity Dawkins walked beside her mother, holding her hand. There was a mulish, disappointed look on her pudgy face, and the glance she sent Miss Hadley from her pale blue eyes was pure malice.

Twelve

CELIA WENT DOWN to dinner that evening in a much happier frame of mind than she had been in for several days, and she knew very well why. It was because Viscount Drummond had spoken to her that afternoon, and although it had been an innocuous conversation, he *had* talked to her. He had even said he wished she could have won the prize. She hoped this new state of affairs would continue, but she could not be sure. The viscount was volatile as well as occasionally outrageous.

When she entered the drawing room, she saw the duke and his bride were joining the guests this evening. And was it her imagination, or was there a little pall cast over the company? Conversation was muted as the new arrivals moved among them all, exchanging a few words with each, like royalty conferring a tremendous boon. Celia went to her uncle's side.

"Did you have a pleasant afternoon, my dear?" that gentleman inquired, manfully interrupting a technical conversation with his friend. "I understand there were some real goings-on in the old wing."

"It was most enjoyable, although I'm sorry I didn't win."

"I see Kendall has returned home with his new duchess," Mr. Stark said glumly. "Won't be long now before Dolly flees to London or the dower house. I'll be right behind her. Never saw such a Friday-faced woman as Eunice Farrington in my life."

Her uncle chuckled, and Celia warned, "Shh! She'll hear you!"

"Uncle. Mr. Bell, is it not? I hope my memory serves me right," the duke said as he arrived, his bride on his arm. This lady inspected Celia carefully from the top of her chignon to the tips of her slippers before she condescended to nod slightly.

Celia pinched her uncle when she saw the duke staring at her.

"Your Grace. Duchess. May I present my niece, Miss Celia Anders?" Bell said, waving a careless hand.

As Celia curtsied, the new duchess frowned a little. "I don't believe we know any Anderses, do we, my love?" she asked. "No, I am positive we do not."

"But you do now," Dudley Bell told her, his face unsmiling. "I understand that you have been traveling abroad. Did you go to Greece? I have so wanted to go there myself."

Celia let her mind wander as the duke regaled her uncle with a detailed account of their travels. The duchess appeared to hang on his every word, but Celia caught her in a small yawn. She looked away quickly. Annoying as she found it, there was something about the lady that made one want not to offend her.

Shortly after, when the new arrivals moved on, Drummond came in with his godmother on his arm. Celia was surprised to see how subdued Dolly Farrington appeared this evening.

When they went in to dinner, she saw the dowager had been placed on her son's right hand, while his bride reigned supreme at the other end of the long mahogany table.

How horrid it must be to be displaced like that after all the years you had held sway there, Celia thought. It did not appear the dowager minded very much, though, for her silvery laugh sounded occasionally above the chink of crystal and plate, and the subdued conversation of the guests.

She was disappointed the viscount did not seek her out after dinner. There were to be no games this evening, nor any dancing. Instead, it passed in more conversation and a few quiet card games, due no doubt to the new duchess's wishes.

Celia wondered if the guests were looking forward to the end of their stay at Castle Wentworth in a way they had not before this afternoon. Then, startled, she realized all of them would be there only another week, and she did not wonder why she suddenly felt so depressed.

She looked across the drawing room to where Drummond was in conversation with Earl Castleton. All trace of his disguise was gone, and as he stood there, she admired his crisp dark curls, that handsome profile, and his impeccable evening dress—trying to memorize everything about him for that time when she would see him no more. Then she scoffed at herself. For someone unromantic, she was behaving in a very stupid way. She had always known she had no future with such as he; why did she suddenly regret that?

He turned then and caught her staring at him, but to her surprise he did not smile, pleased he had caught her out. Instead, he frowned. Confused, she looked down to where her gloved hands were clasped in her lap.

"Isn't this the most deadly time?" the dowager whispered as she took the seat next to Celia. "I should not say so, of course, but I have found my son's bride has that general effect on company.

Kendall admires it. He says she is exactly the sort of woman he required." Dolly Farrington sighed. "She is very good. Very moral. Most pious. You must not think I do not know her worth, Miss Anders, and respect her for it."

She sounded not only a little worried that Celia would think just that, but depressed as well, and Celia smiled in sympathy even as she wondered why the dowager would be so frank. She had never been so before.

Encouraged, the dowager went on. "If only she were not such a bore as well! But then, Kendall is, too, so they are well matched. Neither Archibald—my late husband, you know—nor I could ever figure out how he came by it. But perhaps it is one of those unfortunate traits that crops up every few generations or so?"

She sighed again as she inspected the inhabitants of the drawing room, almost as if she were looking for something—or somebody, Celia thought.

"Forgive me, ma'am, but is there anything wrong? Can I help you in any way?"

Dolly Farrington turned to her, studying her face as if trying to gauge her sincerity. Finally she took a deep breath and said, "It is not known by anyone here, but I am missing the ruby pendant I wore last evening. Perhaps you remember seeing it?"

At Celia's nod, she continued. "I heard the gossip about Miss Hadley and completely discounted it. Her grandmother is one of my dearest friends. But now I have to wonder. You see, I did not lock the pendant away with my other jewels last night before I went to bed. That was careless of me, but I was tired, so I merely swept it into one of the drawers of my dressing table. Reminded of that as I was dressing for dinner this evening, I looked for it, but it was not there. Tell me, Miss Anders, do you think Miss Hadley is a thief?"

"I cannot believe it of her even though I did not know her before we met here. And she seemed so sincere when she asked my advice about the gossip—so undone by it. Is she that good an actress? I would not say so from her performance in the play."

"I do not know what I should do," the dowager confided. "I shall not mention this to Kendall and Eunice just yet, for the pendant was left to me by my mother and is not part of the estate. I shall miss it dreadfully if it never comes to light, however. It is all I have to remember her by.

"You know, my dear, this party has not been anywhere near as successful as others I have given, and I have to wonder why. Can it be this horrid, lingering gossip that is going around? Of course, one must always expect some of that. But this time it seems so malicious. So persistent."

"Did Mrs. Grey ever come to you about Lady Powers and Lord Manchester?" Celia could not help asking. "She told me she intended to do so."

Dolly Farrington smiled for the first time since sitting down. "Indeed she did. She was so righteous and indignant, I could not help laughing. Everyone except our tattletale and Mrs. Grey knows Louisa and Alastair have been lovers for years.

"But what if there isn't a tattletale? Could it be Mrs. Grey is spreading all these stories herself? I don't know her or her husband at all and asked them to come only because they are related to Kendall's bride."

"I suppose she could be," Celia said slowly. "Yet I have the feeling there is someone else, someone I suspect I should know about but cannot name. And I am sure Mrs. Grey never stole your pendant.

"I wish I could do more to help you, dear ma'am. You have been so kind, inviting me here. I have enjoyed it more than I can say, and I will never forget your goodness."

The dowager hugged her close for a moment. "My dear child, it is a pleasure and a delight to have you here.

"But now I must stop monopolizing you and go and see if I can't reconcile my dear Cassie to Viscount Drummond. She was so shocked this afternoon by the state of his undress, I cannot tell you."

Celia rose as well, to wander over to where Harriet Hadley was talking to Duke Ainsworth and Earl Castleton. Minutes later, when the gentlemen turned away, Celia whispered, "I must talk to you in private. May I come to your room after everyone has gone to bed?"

Miss Hadley stared before she said all in a rush, "Oh, have you found out who is spreading the gossip about me, Miss Anders?"

The eager light on her face removed all Celia's suspicions that she herself might be the guilty party, and she was sorry when she had to say, "No, it is about something else that I would speak to you. Something equally important. May I come, then?"

Miss Hadley drooped a little but nodded, and Celia left her as Bogle and the footmen brought in the long-awaited tea trays.

Celia waited until she was sure every lady had dismissed her maid that night before she left her room and walked down the corridor to knock on Harriet Hadley's door. It opened promptly, and she slipped inside to put her candle down on a table.

The dowager's story was soon told, while Miss Hadley's expression grew more and more horrified.

"But how perfectly dreadful," she whispered, staring around as if the entire company, fast asleep in the castle, were listening. "But why do you come to me about it?" she asked, her voice shaking. "Is it to *accuse* me?"

"No, please do not disturb yourself," Celia said quickly. "But I think we might just find the pendant here in your belongings. No, do not look so! What I mean is, why wouldn't whoever is talking about you, having taken the pendant, put it here for your maid to find, perhaps? Then you would be truly undone. I assume, you see, it was not stolen for its value."

"Now I understand," Miss Hadley said slowly. "But what can I do?"

"I suggest we search for it right now. I'll help you. Unless you are too tired, that is. I suppose we could do it in the morning."

"No, let us begin. I'd never sleep a wink, else," Miss Hadley said as she went to light another branch of candles. "I'll start with the drawers. Perhaps you might go through the armoire?"

Celia began to inspect the gowns that hung there, being careful to feel in all the pockets. If her theory was correct, the pendant would be easily found, for it would not suit the vicious thief's purpose if it remained lost.

There was nothing in Miss Hadley's extensive wardrobe of evening and carriage gowns and habits. She reached up to the shelf above them to take down the bandboxes placed there. Behind her, she could hear Miss Hadley muttering to herself as she turned out drawer after drawer to paw through her petticoats and shifts, cosmetics and stockings.

The bandboxes contained nothing but an assortment of attractive bonnets, and wearily now, Celia knelt to inspect the lady's footwear.

It was in the toe of one of a pair of kid morning sandals that the jewelry came to light. Celia had often seen Miss Hadley wearing those sandals, and so, no doubt, had the thief. She held up the pendant and chain, calling softly to the young woman as she did so.

Miss Hadley looked distraught as the sparkling ruby caught the candlelight. "So it is true, and you were right. I wonder who it is who hates me so much, and why?" she whispered. "But whatever am I to do?"

Celia made up her mind in a minute. "I think we should take the pendant to the dowager right now," she said.

"But it's so late! She'll be fast asleep!"

"No doubt, but I am sure she will be glad to be awakened when she sees what we have found. She was so upset when it went missing, for the pendant used to belong to her mother and is dear to her."

Miss Hadley looked down at her dressing gown, and Celia said, "No, we don't have time to change. But don't worry. There won't be anyone to see us this late at night. Besides, think how grand it will be to tell the dowager of your innocence right away."

Thinking fleetingly of Lord Manchester, Celia hoped he would not be roaming the halls this night. She remembered the way to the dowager's rooms from the tour the housekeeper had given, and now she led a still-reluctant Miss Hadley directly there.

There was no answer to her first soft knock, and she was forced to knock again harder.

Dolly Farrington was indeed delighted to be roused from a restless sleep, and when she saw the pendant she gave a little cry of joy. Miss Hadley begged her to believe she had had nothing to do with the loss of the jewelry, nor any idea how it had come to be found in her slipper. Celia was quick to explain her theory of how it had arrived there.

"How clever you are, Celia," the dowager said, her voice admiring as she settled back on her pillows. "Do sit down, girls," she added, patting the bed on either side of her. "We have much to discuss."

She looked so much more alive now that her beloved pendant had been returned to her, and her eyes sparkled as she added, "Now, I suggest we keep this a secret among ourselves. Only the three of us know about it, and someone might just give themselves away when there is no hue and cry about its disappearance. And if that doesn't work, perhaps they shall when they see me wearing it again."

"But what if they do this another time?" Miss Hadley dared to ask, her voice rising a little hysterically. "What if other things are stolen and the theft laid to my door again? I should never be able to live it down, and my father will be so cross!"

The dowager laid a comforting but also steadying hand on her arm. "My dear, nothing like that will happen, for I shall see to it.

"Has there been any other gossip I have not heard of?" she asked next, looking from one to the other. "I do feel, somehow, these things are connected. I know of the Powell-Manchester affair, of course."

Miss Hadley stole a quick glance at Celia's face and reddened slightly when she found herself being gravely considered.

"Please tell us," Celia said quietly.

"Well, for a while there was quite a bit of talk about you, Miss Anders, although it seems to have died down now," the blonde confessed.

Celia wondered why the dowager looked so apprehensive even as she said, "And that talk was . . . ?"

"That there was something in your background that made you a most ineligible guest here," Miss Hadley confessed in a rush, hanging her head so she would not have to look into Celia's clear eyes. "But no one seems to know what that could be, although Mrs. Grey suggested a number of things. I think the gossip began because you not only drove to Bath with Viscount Drummond, you stayed beside him all day. In fact, I was sure one of the twins started the talk out of pique and jealousy."

Celia was confused. What could such a rumor possibly mean?

Before she could ask, the dowager said, "That bit of gossip is so vague it is meaningless. There has been no other talk?"

When the girls shook their heads, she smiled again and dismissed them, after thanking them fervently for their help. As they went to the door, candles in hand, she called after them, "Now, remember! Not a word to anyone, girls."

As much as she liked and revered Dolly Farrington, Celia had no intention of obeying her in this instance. Instead, after bidding a grateful Miss Hadley good-night at the door of her room, she went to her own and sat down at the escritoire to write a note.

She would give it to the maid in the morning, and then she would feel more at ease, she decided as she sanded it and prepared to seal it. For there was no way she was going to be able to solve this nasty mystery herself, nor did she think the dowager and Miss Hadley would be much help. But somehow she was sure Viscount Drummond would be, and it was to him her note was addressed.

That gentleman received it the following morning

before he even left his room, and he spent quite a bit of time reading it and wondering why it had been written.

Surely it was singular for Miss Anders to write begging a private interview. An interview, moreover, she seemed determined to keep secret from everyone at the castle, up to and including the servants, if the location she suggested was any clue. And she gave no reason for the tryst, except to say it concerned a matter of grave importance.

The viscount had received mysterious notes before from determined, eager misses as he maneuvered his elusive way through the rock-strewn channels of bachelorhood. But somehow he did not think Celia Anders was intent on capturing him as a matrimonial prize. The tone of her note was serious, and although it contained a definite hook, intriguing him as it did, he did not think she had intended it that way. Indeed, the words she had used made him think she had been frightened when she wrote them.

Accordingly, he did not hesitate to jot down a short reply agreeing to the meeting, which he gave his valet to deliver.

"Place it only in Miss Anders's hands, Petson," he ordered as he tucked her note safely away.

Mr. Petson bowed, although he wondered what his unpredictable master was up to now. He sighed. After all the effort of getting the viscount to appear a creditable sculpture—and a lot of work that had been, too!—he had been looking forward to a little peace and quiet. For at least a few days. Alas, he thought, that it was not to be.

Thirteen

I⸀T CAME ON to rain hard shortly after twelve, and a nasty wind had blown up, but somehow Viscount Drummond was certain none of that would deter Miss Anders from reaching their rendezvous. He himself donned a waterproof cloak and made sure he had a large umbrella before he left the castle by a little-used door, to make his way through the sodden gardens.

He had seen once before the woodland glade deep in the woods she had mentioned in her note. It was not a popular spot, not that they would have to worry about being interrupted today, he thought as one foot encased in a shining boot slipped into a muddy puddle. Petson is not going to appreciate any of this, the viscount told himself as he rounded a corner and saw the little three-sided shelter ahead of him that was his destination. He was not at all surprised to see Miss Anders was already there, clad in a warm-looking navy cloak, the hood pulled up to protect her hair.

Her face lit up in relief when she saw him, and the biting comment that had sprung to his lips about how unwise she was to lure men off to trysts in the lonely woods died aborning.

"Thank you for coming," she said fervently. "Somehow I was sure you would not fail me."

He took her hand and helped her to a seat on the bench at the back of the shelter, away from the lash of the windblown rain that was still trying to reach them.

Her tale was not soon told, for he interrupted her many times, but at last she fell silent, her large hazel eyes fixed on his face. Almost, he mused, as if she thought he could solve the puzzle in an instant. No doubt he should be flattered.

"Tell me, Miss Anders, why did you come to me for help?" he asked quietly. "And why do you want to be involved in this anyway? It is most unsuitable for a woman."

"I came to you because I knew I could trust you," she said after a moment, for she had not expected that question. "And how can I help being involved? I am being gossiped about, too. I refuse to discuss why my being a woman makes it unsuitable for me to try to stop it.

"But I also came to you because I am afraid. Afraid that this is not over, that there will be more evil done. And I have the strangest feeling that I know who is doing this, yet I cannot put a name to the person.

"Have you ever dreamed you were running and running, trying to catch someone? Someone who remained elusive, just out of sight, around a corner, behind a veil? It is like that for me."

He shrugged, as if he did not understand such a feminine fancy. "But even so, which of our fellow guests appeal to you most as the culprit, Miss Anders? You must have some opinion."

For the briefest moment, her little smile peeked out. He felt as if the sun had suddenly appeared, and was as quickly gone.

"I am afraid to say, for the ones I suspect most are the ones I like least. Mrs. Grey, for example. What a nasty woman she is, with her horrid talebearing. And I'm not fond of her husband. As for

146

the others, it doesn't seem possible any of them could be guilty, but that kind of thinking won't get us anywhere."

"I dislike Mrs. Dawkins the most," he confided. "She should have been strangled at birth, she is so tiresome, going on and on as she does about that ghastly brat of hers."

He stopped suddenly to stare at Celia. As she returned that stare, her eyes widened, and for several seconds there was only the sound of the rain beating on the crude wooden roof and the moan of the wind.

"What are you thinking? No, that cannot be," Celia said at last. "Charity Dawkins is only a child!"

Her voice died away and he nodded. "Yes, if it is she, she is very young for evil. But I have never thought only adults capable of it. When I was at Eton, most of the others there were boys like me, made up of good and bad. But there was one boy I always avoided. Somehow I knew the devil had his soul. I do not consider myself fanciful when I say that, even after all these years. Especially now, when I know what he became as a man."

Celia was speechless, but he saw how tightly she was clasping her gloved hands together in her lap, and the little frown she wore on her forehead. He wished he could smooth it away.

Pushing that ridiculous urge aside, he made himself say, "For argument's sake, let us assume it is little Charity who is doing all these things. She certainly has the opportunity, left alone as much as she is. And have you ever noticed the way she wanders through the halls all the time, peering into rooms, watching us all? It is most disconcerting, and I know I'm not the only one she has been bothering. Several other guests have mentioned that unpleasant habit of hers."

"Yes, I've seen her doing that, too," Celia admitted. "But she always has a book under her arm as if she were looking for a quiet room to read in."

"With a hundred to choose from, I cannot see her dilemma," Drummond remarked dryly.

"But why would she do such a thing? Even if she is, as you say, evil—and I cannot agree to that theory myself, sir—she would not cause trouble just because she was bored."

"Wouldn't she just," he murmured, but Celia ignored him as she went on. "Perhaps she has overheard people making derogatory comments about her. She's not a very appealing child, is she, poor thing? And those comments might well make her angry."

He nodded, looking grim now. "And, of course, being besotted, her mother would take her side. Perhaps that is the secret, Celia!"

He sounded so excited, Celia decided to ignore his most improper use of her name.

"No doubt Mrs. Dawkins has been telling Charity how peerless and wonderful she has been since birth. Why, perhaps she even thought she would be included in the party. Don't you remember how upset she was that first morning when she discovered her daughter wasn't even to take her meals with us? And how she kept insisting she join us?"

He looked thoughtful for a moment, and Celia wondered what he was thinking.

"Perhaps Mrs. Dawkins has always excused her daughter's naughty ways because she did not see them for what they were," he went on at last. "Children can be cruel. They have to be taught not to hurt others. But I would wager Charity Dawkins has never had lessons of that sort, wouldn't you?"

"What shall we do?" Celia asked, her eyes searching his face. "We certainly can't accuse her when we have no proof. She may very well be innocent, and you know it."

"Perhaps, but she *fits* so well. So we must get the proof. I think we should keep an eye on her as much as possible. I'll set my valet to watch as well. If she is guilty, she is sure to redouble her efforts when she sees the dowager wearing her pendant again, and Miss Hadley not accused of stealing it. We must hope she is not clever enough to become more cautious instead."

"*Brrr,*" Celia said, rubbing her arms. "How frightening this is, even thinking a child of that age could be so devious, so determined to wreak havoc among us. It makes my blood run cold."

"Since that is the case, I shall not tell you about another scheme I have in mind that might shed some light on the subject."

"But that is most unfair. After all, I was the one who brought this problem to your attention in the first place."

He reached out to take her hands in his, and his face grew serious. "Yes, you did, but what I intend to do is better accomplished by a man. You see, I'm not sure you might not try to take care of it yourself, if you knew of it."

"With reservations, I bow to your judgment," Celia made herself say evenly, wishing he would let her go so her breathing could return to normal.

"Tell me, what do you make of this tale being spread about you?" he asked next. "Have *you* ever said anything about Charity Dawkins that might make her angry with you? Turned up your nose at her? Frowned, perhaps?"

"No, none of those things. Honestly, I never have because I pitied her so, I suppose."

"You are such a saint, ma'am?" he drawled.

"Oh, it is not that she does not irritate me with her sullen ways, and I have often thought what a strange child she is, but I never told anyone that. Being a stranger here, I have hesitated to confide in anyone."

"Is there something in your background that might be thought offensive to persons of quality?" he persisted, glad she had at least confided in him.

Celia tried to pull her hands away, but he would not let her go.

"Answer me," he ordered in a quiet voice that was nonetheless impossible to deny.

"I have no idea," Celia said, her color high. "I don't see how there could be when my uncle is everywhere received."

"I suggest you tell him what is being said, and ask his advice," Drummond suggested. "It may be it is only something our gossip made up out of whole cheese. But even if that were to be the case, there are entirely too many people who would be sure to say that where's there's smoke, there's fire. I would not have such a cloud hanging over you."

"Why?" Celia asked. She saw his face change, become more intent, and she wished she had held her tongue.

"Because I care for you," he said. There was a long pause before he added, "You are a very nice woman, and you deserve better than you have been served here. And, I suppose I am concerned because I hate injustice."

Celia wished he had not qualified his answer, for she liked the first sentence of it best. She looked down to where their hands were clasped together, and bit her lip. His hands were warm and strong and comforting, just as she knew his arms would be

150

if he were to put them around her again. She forced herself to look away from him.

"It is kind of you. Thank you," she made herself say. "Perhaps I will ask Uncle Dudley, although I hate to upset him. He has said so little about my mother and father over the years, it does not seem quite right to badger him about them now."

He released her at last, but only to draw her to her feet. "Of course, you must do as you think best," he said.

Celia took a small step away from him, then another. He smiled, a rueful smile that transformed his face. "I do not think it wise for us to return to the castle together," he said. "You go ahead. I'll take a different route later."

She nodded and bent to pick up her umbrella. As she straightened, he reached out and pushed her hood back so he could trace a path down her jawline from her ear to her chin with his thumb. Startled, she stood very still as that thumb caressed her lips, pulling the lower one down a little. Slowly. So slowly.

As soon as he took his hand away she left him, pulling her hood up again and hurrying down the path. But she knew his brooding gaze watched her go, and it was all she could do to keep moving away, when what she wanted to do was run back to him as fast as she could.

Alone in the shelter, Drummond wondered at himself and the words he had almost but not quite said. Of course, he knew he liked Celia Anders. But why had he wanted to say more than that, to tell her he loved her as he had never thought to love? He, who had never imagined he would say those most damning, particular words?

At last he started back to the castle. And as he walked, bracing himself against the wind, he made himself think of Charity Dawkins. He knew he wasn't wrong. Children were capable of a great deal more than adults gave them credit for. And she was all of twelve or so. Fully old enough to be up to the vilest kind of mischief, if that was how she was bent. The trick would be to prove it, but he did not think that would be at all difficult as long as she did not know she was suspected. He must warn Celia not to give the game away.

And thinking of her again effectively drove Charity Dawkins right from his mind.

Mr. Petson was just as disapproving as the viscount had known he would be when he saw the state of those boots he had polished only that morning to gleaming perfection. Nor could he approve the sodden cloak he removed from his master's shoulders.

He tried to make his sniff especially meaningful, and was startled when William Welburn turned to stare at him and say, "But of course!

"Tell me, Petson, are the rumors I heard earlier today about the butler's illness true?"

"Indeed, m'lord. Mr. Bogle has been forced to take to his bed. From his symptoms, I suspect food poisoning. But how he could get that when he eats exactly the same food as everyone else in the servants' hall, I can't say."

He shook the mistreated cloak as the viscount said, "But perhaps there is something only he eats? Or drinks?"

Petson's eyes narrowed. "I have heard he keeps a special decanter in his pantry, with Her Grace's permission. He suffers from rheumatism, and a nip now and then seems to ease it."

"Get me that decanter, if you would, Petson," Drummond ordered.

His valet's brows rose alarmingly, and he added, "I suspect the cause of Mr. Bogle's illness is in it. I'll throw out the contents and replace them with some fresh spirits, and we shall see if he does not make a miraculous recovery. Oh, and by the way, it was you who put me in mind of yet another victim."

Seeing Mr. Petson did not understand him in the least, Drummond told him everything that was happening in the castle, and his suspicions that Charity Dawkins was behind it all. "Bogle has made no secret of his dislike for the child, so you see, if he has been sniffing at her in that disapproving way all you chaps seem to know instinctively and use so effectively, she might well have decided she must pay him back."

To Drummond's surprise, his valet did not protest the little girl's involvement as Celia Anders had. Instead, he said, "Yes, she's a nasty piece of work, she is. But where would someone like her get poison, sir?"

"Any number of places. From the gardener's shed, or the kitchen. Most cooks keep a supply on hand for the rats. And some of her mother's cosmetics would serve in a pinch."

He told Petson then to watch Charity Dawkins, and he asked him to bring Mrs. Dawkins's maid to him the following morning.

The valet nodded and went away to do his best to restore William Welburn's raiment to its former magnificence.

Mary Motts was most reluctant to visit Viscount Drummond when informed he wanted to see her by Mr. Petson, even though she coveted the guinea that was offered for her time. She might be only a raw country girl, she told herself, but she 'ad 'eard about them there lords. Some o' them 'ad peculiar ideas, they did, an' she was a good girl, she was. On

153

the other hand, a guinea was a lot of money. Finally, after getting Mr. Petson to promise he would not leave her alone with his master, she agreed to the visit. Mr. Petson followed her, his face a study of indifference. But to himself as he watched Miss Motts's ample bottom sway from side to side as she climbed the stairs, and remembering her shining, homely face, he had to smile. That she could suspect that anyone as fastidious as Viscount Drummond could have designs on her showed she was truly an optimist.

Miss Motts soon learned how wrong she had been when m'lord began to question her. She became alarmed, then frightened, and as she continued to refuse to answer him she twisted her apron in nerveless fingers.

"Come, come, Miss Motts! There is no need for this coyness," Drummond said, favoring her with a frown since his smiles had gotten him nowhere. "No one will know you have spoken to me."

"I can't say, sir. I can't," she whispered. "Please don't ask me no more."

"Are you afraid of Charity Dawkins?" he thought to ask softly. "Well, are you?"

She paled, but she nodded before she looked around as if to make sure no one had seen her.

"Are you afraid of what she might do to you if she found out you had been speaking to me? Is that why you will not answer my questions?"

A sob was the only reply, for Miss Motts had buried her face in her apron. Mr. Petson came forward and led her to a seat, patting her on the back and whispering to her. In only a few more minutes she was a great deal more at ease, and cautiously, Drummond began to question her again.

To his vast disappointment, she did not know anything specific that could be laid to Charity

Dawkins's door, but she had her suspicions. There had been the family cook back in Northumberland who had suddenly been taken ill with vomiting. She had left the Dawkinses' employ, but Mary had seen her on one of her rare days off, looking as healthy as she ever had. And it was then she had remembered how the cook had often scolded Charity for stealing cookies and other sweets.

"An' Miss Dawkins 'as a way o' lookin' at yer," Mary Motts admitted, wringing her hands again. "Nasty look it is, too. Puts shivers right up an' down yer spine, it do."

"It is unfortunate you must spend so much time with her, then," Drummond said smoothly.

"Well, but that I don't, sir. She don't seem ter want me with 'er, an' I'm jest as glad. 'Sides, I've a deal ter do, takin' care o' 'er ma an' 'er. No, she's off by 'erself most days, although 'er ma don't know it. An' I'm not about ter tell her, no, sirree!"

Eventually, Miss Motts was dismissed, clutching her guinea, and sped on her way by the viscount's assurances that little Miss Dawkins would never hear of their meeting from him.

Drummond was feeling very pleased with himself now that he had some information that confirmed his belief in Charity Dawkins's guilt. And he had replaced the liquor in Mr. Bogle's decanter, so there was another plot foiled. Still, he wondered as he strode to the stables, who would be next? And how could he protect his darling godmother, whom he was very sure was high on the list of people Charity did not like.

His face grew grim as he considered his options. It was then he decided that as soon as he had a single piece of positive proof, he would tell the dowager, and make sure the Dawkinses left the castle the very same day.

It was of course unfortunate that he had not thought to ask Miss Motts if Charity Dawkins was interested in the gossip that was going around the castle. Certainly the maid had not volunteered that information, for her part in spreading the scandal at Charity's suggestion did not put her in a very good light.

But if Drummond had known of it, he would have been able to act at once, something he was to regret a great deal in future days.

Fourteen

WHEN FINALLY CELIA had been able to tear her thoughts from William Welburn and the way he had acted in the shelter, she decided she would not speak to her uncle. She told herself there was no need, that it was only gossip, just as it had been about Miss Hadley. Why distress the dear man. He was having such a wonderful time, spending hours with his crony discussing idea after idea. He positively beamed with good humor when she saw him, and he was so deep in his theories, she wasn't even sure she could get his attention if she tried.

Instead, she considered Charity Dawkins. She still could not make herself believe the child was responsible for the gossip and the thefts, but Drummond did believe it. She decided she would suspend judgment until there was some real proof, for or against.

The morning after their meeting in the woods, she had spent more time at the play rehearsal watching the little girl at the back of the hall than she had the performance. But there was very little need for her anymore, for everyone was becoming letter perfect in their roles. Even Charles Danforth had settled down, although his petulant face showed his disapproval of any vehicle so pedestrian as the dowager duchess's little mystery and farce.

As soon as the rehearsal was over, Celia had followed Charity from the hall, much to the viscount's disappointment. He had been looking forward to telling her exactly what he had discovered about Miss Dawkins, and the butler's mysterious illness as well.

Celia had no luck trailing the little girl, for Charity disappeared behind the baize door that led to the servants' part of the castle. Celia realized she was probably going for a meal in the housekeeper's room, and since she could hardly hang about the hall waiting for her to reappear, she shrugged and went off on her own pursuits. It had occurred to her that it might be wise to warn Miss Hadley she must not act any differently now that the dowager's pendant had been found and returned to her.

Dolly Farrington, meanwhile, was having a long conversation with her son and his bride, an occasion she considered more a chore than a pleasure.

"As I have told you both, I would never have given a house party if I had suspected you would return home during it. I am aware you yourselves would not invite these particular people—with the exception of your relatives, Eunice. Come to think of it, I wouldn't invite a lot of them again, but that's nothing. I always feel this way after people have been and made a long stay. Perhaps there is something to the saying 'Absence makes the heart grow fonder'?"

"Well, it's all water over the dam now, Mother," Kendall said, patting her knee and smiling at her. "When did you say the guests would be leaving?"

"The end of the week. The evening before they are to go, I've invited most of the neighborhood in to see the play they have been rehearsing, and to enjoy a late supper. Of course, I shall bear the expense of the champagne."

"Do not be so ridiculous, Mother! As always, the wine is my responsibility."

Eunice Farrington, who had opened her mouth to commend the dowager for recognizing her duty, said instead, "I am truly sorry you thought to have amateur theatricals, dear ma'am. It is not at all the kind of thing I can bring myself to approve for Castle Wentworth. No, indeed. But I am sure it was only your excessive goodness that allowed you to be persuaded to forego your usual good taste in this instance."

Dolly Farrington smiled. If the duchess had known her better, she would have braced herself.

"I do assure you it is a most unexceptional play, Eunice. Not a swear word in it. And although there is a murder, it takes place offstage, and there is no rape. You may be easy.

"But I must say, if you mention my goodness one more time, I shall be forced to scream. There are no *degrees* of goodness, any more than there are *degrees* of virginity. You are either good or virgin, or you're not."

The duchess was ashen as she rose and said to her husband, "I really cannot remain and listen to such—such talk as this. I must ask you to excuse me, my love."

Her back was very stiff as she made her way to the door, and closed it behind her with a decisive snap.

"Mother," the duke said, forgetting all his intentions to have a pleasant meeting, "do you deliberately *try* to upset Eunice?"

"It's good for her," the dowager told him, a twinkle in her eye. "She is so stodgy—why, she acts older than I do."

"Everyone over the age of twelve acts older than you," he retorted.

"Why, Kendall, darling, what a lovely thing to

159

say. No, no, do not get excited! You are turning quite purple. I wasn't teasing you, I *meant* it."

She sighed before she said, "I am sorry. Please ask Eunice to forgive me, dear. And tell her I am off to London next week. That will cheer her up. I must find my own place in town now that you are married. And when I return to Wiltshire, I intend to live in the dower house. Don't worry. I am sure we shall all rub along very well as soon as we are not living in each other's pockets."

The duke tried to joke about the impossibility of that in a castle of a hundred rooms, but secretly he was relieved. He knew his wife did not like his mother, nor approve of her, and although he could not agree since he did truly love her, maddening as she was, he had to admit life was a great deal calmer when Dolly Farrington was somewhere else.

That evening, the dowager wore her ruby pendant, but although both she and Harriet Hadley looked at everyone's face very carefully, neither lady could discern any guilty start or change of expression. Even Mrs. Grey, whom Miss Hadley, as Celia had, secretly wished were the guilty party, was her usual boring and vindictive self.

Drummond came to Celia's side as soon as the gentlemen rejoined the ladies after dinner. Drawing her a little distance away from the other guests, he sat down beside her on a sofa and proceeded to tell her the things he had discovered.

"How clever it was of you to question the maid, sir," she said, her voice admiring. "Was that the scheme you told me about that you said would be better handled by a man?"

He grinned down at her, and Celia felt her heart-beat quicken. "As it turned out, it might have been easier for you. I had a devil of a time getting her to tell me anything at all. She seems to be terrified of Miss Charity."

"But with her testimony, and the butler's illness, you now have positive proof, do you not?"

"Not quite yet, unfortunately," Drummond said a little absently. He was thinking she had lovely skin. It was set off this evening by a pale green muslin gown with a very low neckline, and he was having trouble concentrating. "Until Bogle regains his health, we cannot be sure the poison, if there was any, was in that decanter," he made himself say, focusing on her hazel eyes. "And you must remember, the maid had no proof to give me. Just suspicions much like my own."

Celia looked to where Dolly Farrington was deep in a discussion with Lord Manchester and Lady Powers, and her face sobered. "But if it is true, and it was done deliberately to cause harm, then what of the dowager? We have all heard her rebuff Mrs. Dawkins and refuse to have Charity anywhere near the grown-ups. If Charity is the guilty one, what might she not try and do to her?"

She sounded so distraught, Drummond forgot he was in a crowded drawing room and took her hand in his to squeeze it. "I've considered that; in fact, I'm giving it my fervent attention. But we must have proof before we accuse the child and speed both her and her mother on their way. Although," he added, "I must admit I regret giving her the opportunity to destroy others' lives in the future."

"Yes, that is too bad, but we can hardly bring a child her age before the law. Perhaps when her mother learns of it, she will be able to curb Charity? But how terrible for her when she has adored her for so long."

"She must be told," he said, his voice grim.

"Someone must prevent Charity Dawkins from trying to exterminate her fellows."

Celia became aware of Lady Cassandra's stare, and gently, she removed her hand from the viscount's grasp. He seemed startled, as if he had forgotten he was holding it. Looking around, Celia saw they were being observed by several others in the room, including the new duchess, who did not look as if she approved of such behavior in her drawing room at all. Celia rose and excused herself to Drummond, hoping her color was not too high as she made her way to her uncle's side.

"If Drummond doesn't watch his step, he's going to find himself married before he knows it," Earl Castleton remarked to his cousin, Bartholomew Whitaker.

That gentleman chuckled. "I fear it's much too late to warn him. Why, he's all April and May, although I suspect he doesn't realize it yet."

"But to Miss Anders!" the earl persisted. "Who would have thought it? A nobody really who has never appeared in society. At least I am fairly sure she's never made her curtsy at one of the queen's drawing rooms. And I've never seen her at Almack's. Besides, although I will grant you she's a nice woman, she's no beauty, and she's been at her last prayers for years. What do you suppose got into the man to choose her?"

Bart Whitaker laughed gently at the puzzled note in his younger cousin's voice. For although Jaspar Howland had fallen in love with a beautiful but most unsuitable older woman a few years past, he now sounded truly confounded. It confirmed Bart's suspicion he had forgotten his earlier calf love entirely, and he was glad of it.

"One never knows who will catch a man's fancy, does one?" he said now. "I daresay Drummond has had his pick over the years, but never, until now, succumbed. Miss Anders has her wits about her and a lively sense of humor. I think he is to be congratulated."

Jaspar Howland did not look convinced, but he nodded. "But what of this talk I've heard?" he said. "That bit about there being something in her background that makes her unsuitable? Do you suppose Drummond knows of it?"

"I have no idea. I don't suppose it would matter to him if he did, not now. But I've no intention of passing that gossip on, have you?"

Castleton looked alarmed. "I say, Bart, I'm not that much an idiot. Man's got a terrible temper, just terrible when he's roused, or so I've heard."

He sighed and added, "I'll be glad to be on my way to London in a few days. Especially now that the new duchess has arrived to take over the castle. What an impossible woman Eunice Farrington is!"

"Yes, such a bore, and so unbending and moral. I hope the dowager can avoid her in the future. I suspect her new daughter-in-law would like to murder her, don't you? They are such opposites."

A few minutes later they separated, Mr. Whitaker to a game of whist, and Castleton to raise the twins' hopes by flirting with them both. He had always believed the old saying that claimed there was safety in numbers, so much so, that if they had been triplets, he would have been even more at ease.

The following day was given over to fittings of the ladies' costumes for the play and another rehearsal. Once again Charity Dawkins was in the back of the hall, her pale blue eyes fixed on the stage. It was at the end of rehearsal that Drum-

163

mond, coming down from the stage, saw her there. Unaware she was being observed, Charity stared hard at a particular person and gave a small triumphant smile before she left the room. Confused, Drummond turned to see who she had been looking at, and his eyes narrowed when he saw the footman who had broken his leg earlier busy painting in the background of one of the sets.

Can it be? Drummond asked himself. Could she have done such a thing by herself? And why? Why would she bother with a lowly footman?

Most of the others had left the room when he went over to where the footman was still at work. Fred Givens was an open man with a round, homely face, and he didn't hesitate to admit he had spoken to Miss Dawkins on the first morning of her visit.

"Come into the breakfast room, she did, and took a seat just as if she belonged there, sir," he said as he laid down his paintbrush and stretched his still-splinted leg out straight in front of him. "I told her to make herself scarce. Mr. Bogle ordered me to do so, for she wasn't to eat with the other guests."

"Did she argue with you about it?" Drummond asked.

"Can't say she did," the footman said, frowning as he tried to remember. "Best as I recollect, she just got up and left."

"What happened the morning you broke your leg?" Drummond asked next.

"Still can't figure how that happened," Givens admitted. "I'd cleared the table from breakfast and was going down the stairs with a loaded tray, when I suddenly lost my footing about halfway down. Everything landed with a crash, including me, sir! It was as if I tripped, but there's nothing to trip on there. The drugget is good and tight, and I've been

164

going up and down those stairs for over a year. I had one of my mates check it later, lest someone else take a spill. He didn't find anything."

"Thank you for your information. I think I'll just have a look at those stairs myself."

Givens picked up his paintbrush and grinned. "It would surely be a help to me if you were to find something, m'lord. The other servants have been calling me Flying Fred. Can't say I care for it."

Drummond promised to do his best before he left the hall and went to the baize door that led to the servants' stairs. He went down them slowly, paying careful attention to the middle of the flight. There was nothing there. At the bottom he turned to walk down the hall beside the flight. Suddenly he stopped and leaned close to one particular post at his eye level. On the outside of that post, at the edge of the stair it guarded, was a tiny piece of twine. He picked it up and examined it carefully, and his face was grim as he wrapped it in his handkerchief.

Hidden behind the barely ajar door of the housekeeper's room, Charity Dawkins watched him go back up the stairs. Her pale blue eyes were cold. What had he found? And what did he intend to do with it? she wondered. Could it be he suspected her of tripping the footman? But why would he do that? Why would he even care? Had he spoken to that footman after she left the hall? Learned something?

She followed Drummond slowly up the stairs, so deep in thought she forced one of the maids coming down with a large pile of sheets in her arms to have to flatten herself against the wall to let her go by. The maid glared at her. Fortunately for her, Charity did not notice.

But so what if he'd found a piece of the twine she'd used, she told herself as she went up to her room. There was no way he could accuse *her* of anything. And even if he did, no one would believe him. She was only a little girl. Nice little girls didn't do such things. And Mama would be sure to fly to her defense, screaming and carrying on. Making one of her scenes, Charity reminded herself with a sly grin as she sat down on her bed. A moment later she fell backward, to stare up at the canopy above her, legs dangling over the side.

She'd just have to wait and see what happened, she decided after several minutes of thought. And if Drummond accused her of anything, she'd find out where he got the idea in the first place. Someone had to have said something. Seen something. But who? The dowager? Miss Anders? That stern valet of his, Mr. Petson?

It was a shame. Everything had been going so well. Mr. Bogle was still not below stairs, so he couldn't sniff at her every time she went by him. She chuckled. That rat poison must be pretty powerful. She'd put only a few drops in his decanter.

She frowned a little, remembering. That had been scary. She'd almost got caught in his pantry. Whew!

She'd just put the decanter back where she'd found it when she'd heard Mr. Bogle's voice right outside the door. She'd even seen the doorknob turning. Talk about frightened! There wasn't any-place to hide in the pantry, either. It was lined with cupboards, but those cupboards were filled with china and crystal and plate—bottles of wine as well. There was no room for her. She'd thought of squeezing behind the door when he came in, hoping he wouldn't close it behind him and see her there, when she heard one of the footmen say, "The porter wants to know if he should let a party of travelers inspect the grounds, sir. They've just asked permission."

"With not only the dowager but the duke and his bride in residence? Certainly not," Bogle had declared. "I'll handle this myself. You know how the dowager dislikes these inching cits, pushing in where they've no business to be."

His voice had faded as he spoke, so Charity had known they were moving away. She'd taken a deep, relieved breath before she cautiously let herself out of the pantry to flee to another part of the castle. That had been a close escape, but somehow, as always seemed to happen, she'd come through it with no harm done.

Why, she'd been in and out of all the guests' rooms by now, poking around, looking into their things, with no one the wiser. It was easy after she learned their routines, and found out when their maids and valets were apt to be about. She'd never even had a close call.

But now she'd have to be careful, with Viscount Drummond maybe getting ahold of a piece of that twine. He'd looked so grim, yet kind of satisfied, too. What did that mean?

And there was something else to worry about. How had the dowager's ruby pendant been returned to her with no hue and cry after Miss Hadley? Mama had told her only this morning that the dowager had worn it again last evening. Charity knew how much her mama admired the pendant. She wished she could have given it to her instead of hiding it in Miss Hadley's sandal. But somehow or other, someone had found it and given it back to the dowager. Who had done that? Who?

Maybe she'd better forget putting rat poison in the dowager's morning chocolate. How disappointing! She'd just figured out how to do it when no one was looking. But now it might be too dangerous.

Charity's face assumed its normal blank expression as she pulled a lock of her hair under her nose like a mustache before she began to chew the end of it. This was a habit her mother deplored, but somehow it made it easier for her to think.

It was all that Viscount Drummond's fault she couldn't pay the dowager back for being so mean to her, she told herself. But *he'd* pay, see if he wouldn't. She'd meant to wait until the day the play was to be given to reveal Miss Anders's real background, but she wouldn't wait any longer.

Not anymore. Not now.

Fifteen

ANYONE WHO HAS ever started a fire knows how slow it is to catch at first; what an age before the kindling is safely ablaze. But there comes a time, all at once, when the fire begins to roar, and the smoke from it makes its way up the chimney in a steady stream.

The gossip about Celia Anders was like that. From a few whispered remarks to something everyone in the castle, from the duke and duchess to the lowliest scullery maid, knew, it spread like wildfire. Eventually there were several versions of her history afoot, for as the gossip passed from person to person, it grew and changed as gossip always does.

In most versions, Celia's mother was said to be from a noble family. Her father, on the other hand, was depicted as a groom, footman, tinker, or one of a band of Gypsies. It was claimed that mad with lust, her mother had run away with her unsuitable lover, although whether any wedding had taken place was problematical.

"Imagine," one upstairs maid whispered to another, "an' Miss Anders's a bastard, too! Ain't that *awful?*"

It was thought both parents were dead now, although Mrs. Grey claimed she had heard the Bells' daughter had gone crazy after being forcibly separated from her lover and had to be confined to this day in a cell at the top of her father's house, closely guarded lest she harm herself or others. According to Mrs. Grey, the blackguard in the case had taken every penny of Miss Bell's enormous fortune before deserting her and their child to sail to America. How he had done that, when whatever money Miss Bell might have had was firmly under her father's control, nobody seemed to know. Or care.

"And let that be a lesson to you, my girls," Lady Flowers had told her dumbstruck daughters at the conclusion of Mrs. Grey's recital. "That is what happens to willful misses who think they know better who would suit them for a husband than their parents. An illiterate wanderer? How ghastly!"

But several of the guests refused to accept the gossip without proof. Harriet Hadley was one, David Powers another.

"But think how frightful if it's true, son," Lady Powers said. "And I asked her to call on us in London. Oh, dear!"

Mr. Powers patted her hand. "I suggest we wait and see what the truth may be. Surely it would be most unlike the dowager to invite Celia Anders here if her father was a costermonger and her mother a bawd, now, wouldn't it?"

Like him, most of the younger gentlemen reserved judgment, although Viscount Drummond swore at Duke Ainsworth when that man relayed the news. Throwing down the journal he had been reading, and completely forgetting the coming play rehearsal, Drummond went in search of Celia. Unfortunately, she was nowhere to be found in the castle.

Meanwhile, Lady Cassandra was so upset after hearing the gossip from her niece Drusilla, she decided she must brave the dowager's rooms. She had never done so before, for she knew Dolly disliked receiving anyone before noon.

"You will be good enough to tell Her Grace I am come on a matter of great urgency, Findle," she told the dowager's maid, her face grave and her hands trembling.

"So you've come about that talk that's going around about Miss Anders, m'lady?" the maid said as she admitted her.

"You know?" Lady Cassandra whispered, clutching the lace at her throat.

Findle nodded. "Everyone knows, except the duchess, that is, because she's just now awake.

"Lady Cassandra, Your Grace," she said as she preceded the visitor into the dowager's pretty bedroom.

"Cassie? What on earth?" Dolly Farrington said as she struggled to a sitting position while her maid propped a number of lace-trimmed pillows behind her. "Oh, do not tell me the castle is on fire or anything else horrid! Not this early!"

Lady Cassandra sat down on the bed and captured her friend's hands. "I'm so sorry, Dolly, but you must be told. And although I wish I didn't have to do it, I feel it is my duty, for—"

"Do get on with it," the dowager interrupted. "I hate all these preliminaries that are supposed to cushion the blow. Who has died?"

Her friend recoiled. "Why, no one, of course. What a terrible thing to say!"

The dowager hid a sigh. "What has happened, then?" she asked as patiently as she could. "Out with it."

Lady Cassandra confessed all at last. "I still can't believe what you told me in confidence is now common knowledge," she ended.

"But how did anyone find out?" Dolly asked, her eyes narrowed in thought. "Only I knew of it, until that day in the drawing room when I told you."

"Dolly, I swear I didn't mention it to a soul! On my honor, I swear," Lady Cassandra said, tears coming to her eyes. "Oh, I cannot bear to have you suspect me—"

"Well, of course I don't, goose! You haven't a vicious bone in your body. But someone knew of it besides us. I wonder who? And I wonder why they waited until now to reveal it. It was always such a juicy bit of gossip."

"What shall you do?" Lady Cassandra asked as Findle finished opening all the draperies. The bright sun that streamed into the room seemed to mock her funereal tones.

"I've no idea what I *can* do. Oh, drat!"

When Lady Cassandra looked a question, she added, "How Eunice will smile when she hears this. Then she'll make a point of telling me how unsuitable such a guest is here in the castle, lording it over me as she does so. And then she'll kindly excuse me by saying it is only my age that makes me forgetful of our name. I cannot tell you how often I itch to slap her.

"And Kendall will be so disappointed in me, poor lamb. Although you would think he'd be used to it by now, wouldn't you? And, of course, everyone will talk and talk.

"But mainly, Cassie, I'm concerned for that poor young woman. I never thought anything like this would touch her. Her mother's indiscretion was kept so quiet that very few people were aware of it even at the time."

"What of Drummond? You saw him holding her hand the other night in the drawing room. I was never so shocked."

"Drummond," the dowager said. "I had forgotten him. Yes, and this is the type of thing that might turn him all chivalrous and noble, begging her to marry him so she can have the protection of his name. Bah! Men!"

"Oh, never say so," a horrified Lady Cassandra exclaimed.

"Tell me, Findle, what do you think I should do about this?" the dowager asked, turning to her maid.

Findle ignored Lady Cassandra's indrawn breath. She had been the dowager's confidante for years, and if Lady Cassandra didn't approve of it, that was no great matter. "I see only one thing you can do, Your Grace. You must suggest Miss Anders and her uncle leave the castle today, as soon as they can be packed. I am sure the young lady would agree. It will be so much less painful for her that way, and with any luck she will not even have to see any of the others again."

Dolly Farrington sighed. "Of course you are right, my wise Findle," she said. "Where is Celia Anders now?"

"I understand she begged to be excused from the rehearsal. She said it was too glorious a day to spend indoors."

"Well, then she is safe for a little while. Bring her to me as soon as she returns to the castle. I would tell her about the gossip before anyone else does."

But the dowager was not to be the one who broke the news to Celia, for as she was walking around the lake toward the wood, she heard Viscount Drummond calling her name. She turned toward him, but the smile that was forming on her lips disappeared when she saw his furious face.

"What is wrong?" she demanded before he even reached her. "Is the dowager all right?"

He stopped beside her, his dark eyes searching her face. "This has nothing to do with Her Grace.

But can it be you have not heard the news that is going around this morning?"

"I guess not," Celia said before she waved her hand. "Shall we walk, sir? The sharp breeze makes it cold, standing about."

Absently, the viscount offered his arm.

"I did leave the castle some time ago," Celia confided. "And I saw no one but the maid, for I had breakfast in my room."

She frowned then, remembering that servant's concealed excitement. Not knowing the girl well, she had hesitated to ask about it when it might have been personal. Now she wondered if her reticence had been wise.

"What is this talk, m'lord?" she asked, turning her head to stare up at his frowning face.

"It concerns you and your background. I understand there are several versions going about. You may take your pick. The villain of the piece is your father."

"My father?" Celia echoed, bewildered. "But I told you I know little of him, my mother, either."

"It might have been better if you had questioned your uncle as I suggested. If anyone knows the real story, it will be he."

"Tell me what people are saying. No more roundaboutation, sir," Celia demanded, staring straight ahead now.

Drummond spoke quietly for several minutes. The occasional glance he darted at Celia Anders's calm profile showed only that she had paled somewhat. He would never have been able to guess how upset she really was if it had not been for the death grip she had on his forearm. He wondered if he would be bruised there tomorrow.

"Who would tell such a thing?" she demanded when his voice died away. "Even if it is true, which

174

I find hard to believe, who would be so spiteful, so mean?"

"Charity Dawkins, of course. But why would she attack you?" he wondered. "And how did she find out? She is very young and has lived in Northumberland all her life. And if I didn't know, when my family seat is very near the Bells' in Oxfordshire, how could she?"

Celia shook her head. "I have no idea. It must be someone else."

She stopped then and released his arm. Drummond was not even tempted to rub it, not when he saw the unhappiness in her face. Before he could speak, she said through stiff lips, "Thank you for warning me, sir. I must return to the castle at once and seek my uncle's council."

"You aren't intending to run away, are you?" he asked as he turned to escort her back.

"I'm not sure. But if there is even a grain of truth to these stories, I think it would be best to leave."

"That is the coward's way," he told her.

Stung by the censure she thought she heard in his voice, Celia retorted, "Then I am a coward! Have you thought how unpleasant it would be for me to have to mingle with the other guests now? Ignore their whispers? Their scorn? Go in to dinner on some disapproving gentleman's arm who is cursing his ill fortune? Spend hours with the ladies, especially *dear* Mrs. Grey? Besides, the house party is as good as over. I will not be missed."

"Yes, you will," Drummond said, but she would not look at him. Instead, she hurried her steps.

"I shall miss you more than I can say," he continued. He stopped then and grasped her arms, to keep her near him. "Listen to me, Celia! I won't allow you to go off like this, leaving everyone to believe the stories are true. I won't."

Her brows rose in simulated surprise. "*You* won't? But it is not your place to dictate to me, m'lord. I and I alone shall decide what to do—after I have heard my uncle out, of course."

He shook her a little in pure frustration. "Will you at least promise to speak to me before you make the final decision?" he asked, bending closer. "Surely you owe me that."

She turned her head away. "Very well. Now, please, m'lord, let me go," she whispered. "This is very hard for me. Please."

He released her at once, and she nodded her thanks. The breeze off the lake blew her hood back, and a strand of her chestnut hair came loose from her chignon to whip across her face. She smoothed it back before he could do it for her. Still his eyes searched her face. It was set as any stone. Lifeless. White.

"No matter what is said, no matter the truth, it does not change you, Celia," he told her, and knew he spoke the truth, too. "You are still the same wonderful woman I have come to know. And to love."

"No," she cried, whirling toward him so quickly, her skirts flew out in a bell. "Don't say that! You must not. There can be nothing between us. Not ever!"

Drummond did not have a chance to reply, for she was gone, running up the slope to the castle gardens. He watched her, his face bleak and his hands knotted into fists. He had not meant to tell her he loved her, but the words had tumbled out before he could call them back. And as soon as he had uttered them, he knew them to be true. He loved her. Nothing else mattered.

He should have known when he felt that fury at Ainsworth for telling him everyone was gossiping about her—his love, his love. He should have known by the way he had rushed to find her, to comfort her, let her know he was beside her and wouldn't desert her. He should have known.

Above him, Charity Dawkins stood at a window on the third story of the castle and stared down at him. She saw the unhappiness on his face, the loss written there, and she was so glad, she hugged herself and grinned. Serves him right, she told herself as she watched him walk slowly after Miss Anders, his hands behind his back and his head bent in thought. Teach you, it will, she added before she moved away from the window as her mother came in.

Celia went straight to her uncle's rooms. She looked neither right nor left, nor did she pay any attention to the whispers of the maids and footmen she encountered on her way. Since she had entered the castle by a side door, the footman who was to give her the dowager's message was unsuccessful, for he waited for her in the front hall.

Neither did Celia meet any of the guests. The cast of the play was busy rehearsing, and the others of the party had settled to a morning of gossip in the library or drawing rooms.

The servant who answered her knock started when he saw her, but he went at once to fetch her uncle.

"My dear Celia, what is it?" Dudley Bell said as he came from his bedroom, still holding a sheaf of papers. His niece knew he wanted her to go away so he could continue his study, but she had no intention of doing that.

"Please dismiss the servant, Uncle," she said as quietly as she could. "We have a great deal we must talk about in private."

Mr. Bell peered at her, and something he saw in her face made him quick to wave the servant away.

He put his papers down on a table and beckoned her to take a seat. "What is wrong, Ceely?" he asked as he sat across from her.

"You have not heard the gossip that is going around?" she asked, ignoring his use of her nickname. Then she answered her own question. "But of course you have not. No one would be so crude as to mention it to you. No one but me, that is. But I would have the truth, Uncle, and I think you are the only one who knows it. You see, someone here has been saying things about my mother and father. They say my mother ran away with him, that he was nothing but a tinker or a Gypsy. They even say they never married and I am a bastard."

"Of course you're not a bastard!" Dudley Bell exclaimed. "There are papers to prove your mother married Francis Anders at Gretna Green in 1784."

"That is a relief, at least. But who *was* Francis Anders? Where is he now? How did my mother meet him? And why was there a runaway elopement?"

Dudley looked out the window as he composed his thoughts. He looked years older than he was, the lines of his face showing his distress, but Celia was not tempted to spare him. Instead, she stared at him, prepared to wait as long as it took until he was forced to tell her the truth.

"Your mother was a pretty little girl as a child, with soft chestnut curls and rosy cheeks. I always loved her the best of all my sisters," he began, staring down at his clasped hands. "She was the youngest by far of the family, and I fear we were all guilty of spoiling her.

"When she was just turned sixteen, she formed a

178

fancy for one of my father's footmen. His name was Francis Anders.

"Did you say something, dear?"

Celia shook her head, biting back another exclamation lest her uncle think better of telling her the rest.

"No one thought much of it, as I remember now," he continued. "Many young girls form passions for unsuitable men. But generally they get over it. Your mother did not. And I must say, my father was distraught when he discovered that instead of repulsing her, Anders had so far forgotten himself as to plan secret meetings—kissing and caressing her until it was far too late for them to see reason."

He sighed and drew a deep breath before he continued. "On discovering what was afoot, my father forbade Letty to have anything more to do with him, and to make sure she could not, he discharged Anders. The next morning they were both gone. We did not hear anything for the longest time, for the men my father sent after them found no trace. But eventually, months later, Letty came home. She was emaciated, dressed in ragged clothing—so different from the laughing girl I had known before, I wept."

Dudley Bell sighed. "Yes, I wept, and I hated my father. He would have denied her entrance if she had not been about to give birth. I learned Anders had been unable to find steady work, for he had no references, and, of course, Letty didn't even know how to boil an egg. I don't know how they survived.

"But in the end, Anders sent her back to her family, to spare her, and to give you a chance, my dear. Letty told me that, as she told me how their love had never faltered all those long, hard months. How she had hated to leave him. What a wonderful man he was. I don't know about that. I had known him only as a servant, and that is to say not at all.

"As for where Francis Anders is now, I have no idea. He never came back to Oxfordshire. I often wondered if he knew his Letty had died. But he could not write, you see, so there was no way he could have let us know his whereabouts. And truly, Ceely, your grandfather would have had him horsewhipped, or worse, if he had made any attempt to get close to her again.

"At last, when you began to grow up and look so much like her, my father asked me to take over your care, for he could not bear to see you. You must not hate him, dear. In his own way he had loved Letty more than any of us, and so was more deeply hurt. And I was happy to take care of you, for when you were near, it was like having my sister back with me again."

"Why did I never know this?" Celia asked as he paused and coughed a little. "Why was I never told? *Why?*"

"I thought it best you did not know, and if I was wrong about that, I am sorry. But I did it for your well-being, or so I thought. At the time Letty ran away with her Francis, my father gave out that she was gravely ill. Since she was only sixteen, she had not been presented, and when the time came that she should have been, and had her Season, it was common knowledge she was too sickly. Eventually, people not only stopped talking about her, they forgot her completely, even distant members of the family. What really happened was never known, except to a very few. Dolly Farrington knew, of course, but she, like I, thought your secret safe. How it is that it comes out now, I have no idea. Not through the dowager. She would scorn to gossip about such a thing, and it was she who begged me to let you come, for she said you would be safe here, yet able to have some enjoyment for a change."

Celia was thinking of something else. Now she stared at her uncle and said, "Is all this why Mr. Garfielden suddenly stopped calling on us several years ago?"

Her uncle ducked his head, peering at her shyly. "Well, yes, it was. He had asked my permission to pay his addresses to you, and I felt I had to tell him about your background. I swear I never thought he would just up and decamp like that. After all, you are legitimate, and half a Bell, and he seemed so much in love. But tell me, Ceely, were you hurt when he went away? Did you love him?"

He sounded anxious, and Celia made herself smile and pat his hand. But she could still remember the heartache she had experienced when Andrew Garfielden had abandoned her after showering her with calls and notes and flowers. It was why she had tried to convince herself, when she was eighteen, that she was not romantic.

And perhaps, she told herself now, it was just as well she had learned that lesson then. It was plain to see there would be no romance for her in her lifetime.

Viscount Drummond was absurd. She was sure he had been carried away by chivalry, or impulse, or generosity this morning when he had told her he loved her. But when he had had time to think, he would see as clearly as she saw herself that any liaison between the two of them was impossible.

William Welburn, fourth Viscount Drummond, and a footman's daughter? How ridiculous!

Sixteen

VISCOUNT DRUMMOND FOUND his valet putting away some freshly laundered cravats when he reached his room minutes after Celia ran away from him.

Petson took one look at his frowning, unhappy face, and turned aside so he would not betray the slightest bit of the surprise he felt. The viscount must have heard the gossip. But could he care for Miss Anders so much? Surely only a man in love would look the way he did now.

Of course, there was no way he could inquire, and so, as he took Drummond's cloak, he said, "I've been watching the Dawkins child as you requested, sir. I've not caught her in any mischief yet, but I must tell you that she appears to be following *you* about. She watches you so closely, it's almost as if she's stalking you. And I don't care for that, do you?"

William Welburn shrugged. "I've no idea why she'd bother," he said absentmindedly. "But I'll keep an eye on her, and thank you for your concern."

. He looked at the clock on the mantel and frowned again. It was only eleven. He knew the dowager's habits. Still, he had to speak to her, and privately, at once. Celia had told him there could be nothing between them. He must prove her wrong. To do that, he must have Dolly Farrington's help.

Feeling a little more cheerful, he went to her suite. Findle, being a most superior lady's maid, did not betray by even the flicker of an eyelash how unusual his visit was.

"Do come in, m'lord," she said as she admitted him. "Lady Cassandra has already been here this morning. I knew someone else would come, but I rather thought it would be either the duke or his new bride.

"Lord Drummond, ma'am," she added as she opened the dowager's bedroom door.

"Good gracious, Drummond? I cannot see him, Findle! Send him . . . oh!"

"Oh, indeed, godmother," the viscount said as he stepped inside and shut the door in the maid's face. Findle smiled.

"I do not care that you're not powdered, combed, and painted, ma'am. I have something I must discuss with you, and it can't wait."

"Well, at least sit down," the dowager said, pointing a stern finger. "All your pacing up and down makes me dizzy."

As the viscount obeyed, she went on. "I suppose you have come about Celia Anders. I don't know why you should. She is none of your affair."

"On the contrary, ma'am, she is all of my affair," Drummond replied as he crossed one well-breeched leg over the other. "I intend to marry Celia Anders."

Dolly Farrington closed her eyes and pulled a pillow over her face. Drummond's brows rose as he heard a long-drawn-out moan come from behind that pillow.

"I knew it," she cried as she abandoned her refuge to glare at him. Then she threw the pillow at him as hard as she could. He caught it easily, looking confused.

"Why *can't* you be sensible, William? You *cannot* marry Miss Anders! I doubt anyone would ever receive you again if you did. You are merely suffering an attack of civility, and although it is very nice of you, and certainly more than I expected, it will not do. I am sure Miss Anders would tell you the same thing if she were to learn of it."

"She already has," Drummond announced, his frown returning.

"You have asked her to marry you?" the dowager whispered. "But you cannot know the whole story ... oh, where is Findle? I need my salts!"

Drummond rose to search her bedside table. Handing her the salts, he said, "I am sure you can tell me that story, can't you, ma'am? I would not trouble Celia for it just at present."

The dowager saw by his determined face that he was quite prepared to remain until she was forced by necessity to agree to his demand. She spoke for several minutes, and ended by saying, "So you see, even though they did marry, Anders was nothing but a footman. And because of that, poor Miss Anders is set 'twixt and 'tween, with no place. It is too bad."

"Her place is beside me, and she'll soon learn it," Drummond told her. "I've often thought what society needed most was a good dose of fresh blood. What with everyone marrying their 'own kind,' and sometimes even first cousins, it's no wonder the nobility produces so many half-wits."

"William!" the dowager said in an awful voice.

"It's true and you know it. But here's this lovely woman from the excellent Bell family on her mother's side, and some good solid common English stock on her father's. Perfect!

"Besides, have you ever thought that we were all of us poor nobodies at one time? That it is only the

184

titles bestowed on long-dead ancestors, and our education and inherited wealth, that makes us noble, ma'am? That if fate had twisted things another way, Francis Anders might well have been our king, and you a dairymaid, while I mucked out the stables?"

He paused, but for once his godmother had nothing to say. She only regarded him as if he had suddenly become a half-wit himself. He hid a smile.

"But since Celia refuses to contemplate my suit, I have come to you," he went on. "I am sure if anyone can convince her, it will be you, ma'am. And when I consider the number of years you have been after me to marry, I'm certain you'll be happy to do so. No, don't bother to deny it. You know you asked Miss Hadley and those ghastly Flowers twins here for that express purpose."

"I never—well, perhaps it did cross my mind, but—and instead you choose Miss Anders! Oh, William, you will be so unhappy! How can I make you understand?" she wailed as tears began to fall.

He went to her then to sit on the side of the bed and put his arms around her while she wept. When her tears stopped at last, he handed her his handkerchief.

"You couldn't be more wrong, my darling duchess," he said quietly. "I love Celia. I will always love her, and with her I shall be the happiest of men."

"What do you think you are doing? Get out of my way! I *will* speak to her." The new duchess's raised voice came from beyond the bedroom door. The dowager pushed her godson off the bed, her face a study of apprehension and chagrin.

"Viscount Drummond is with Her Grace, ma'am," Findle said.

That gentleman went and opened the door. "I'm afraid it is not convenient for Her Grace to see you right now, ma'am. I've the prior claim. Perhaps later?"

"I beg your pardon?" the duchess said, sounding stunned.

"Later," he said firmly just before he closed the door in her face.

As her annoyed sputters died away, he took his place again at the dowager's side. "Shall we try once more, ma'am? I intend to marry Celia Anders. I expect you to help me."

Dolly Farrington stared at him, considering. He sounded so positive, so committed. She sensed that if she did not promise to help him, he would manage without her, and the only one who would lose would be herself. For William Welburn would never forgive her. He would make Celia Anders his viscountess, and his godmother would see him no more. And set against her promises to his mother and her wishes for her son was her own very real love for him. *I cannot bear to lose him,* Dolly told herself. *He is too dear to me.*

"Very well, I'll help you," she said at last. "Perhaps you are right, and you will be happy. Lord knows I've seen enough unhappy marriages between social equals. But I warn you, William, this will not be easy."

"I know. Celia is set against it."

"I was not referring to Miss Anders," his godmother said dryly. "But come, let us consider. Somehow or other we must make people believe the gossip is not true."

Drummond's face darkened. "But it is true. Why shouldn't we admit it? I am not ashamed of Celia or her background."

The dowager stifled a sigh. How tiresome men were when they were being noble, she thought. Aloud she said, "Of course *you're* not, but that is not the point. You don't want your Celia to be uncomfortable, do you? Well then, the stories about her must be established as lies. No, no, William, there is no other course.

"Now do go away so I can think. I suggest you go for a long drive—by yourself, mind!—and don't return to the castle till late afternoon. By then I should have all in train.

"Run along, do, and send Findle to me, my dear," she added as if he were no more than two and ten.

The viscount bent to kiss her faded cheek before he obeyed her. Dolly Farrington stared after him until her maid came in and the two of them could put their heads together.

Half an hour later, perfectly coiffed, attired, and discreetly painted, the dowager duchess swept into her new daughter-in-law's rooms and took a seat without even being asked. Before Eunice could speak, Dolly said, "Well, I am sorry, very sorry, to have to tell you, Eunice, that your aunt has been up to mischief here. It is so unfortunate for you. I would never have invited her if I had realized what a dreadful gossip she is. And now she's been spreading stories about Celia Anders, of all people. It will not *do*, Eunice. And how horrid that you are related to her. Or is she perhaps your aunt only by marriage? For your sake, I hope so."

"What are you saying, ma'am?" Eunice Farrington demanded. "These stories—surely they are true."

"But they're not," the dowager said, not even blinking at the lie she told. "Miss Anders's family is known to me. Why, her mother was a special friend. Poor dear Leticia! She never had a Season. But she met Francis Anders in the country, they fell in love, and were married quietly. No one ever heard of it because her father, old Henry Bell, cut up so sharp

187

over it. Besides being his favorite daughter, he did not think Leticia was up to marriage.

"I am sure you know what I mean, Eunice. We are both married women. There is no need for you to color up that way."

"But who *was* Francis Anders?" the duchess asked, happy to be able to change the subject. "I've never heard of any Anders."

"Nor, do I suppose, has anyone else in England. Mr. Anders was an American, over here on business. Americans do not feel as we do about trade, which is why so many of them have such bags of money. He was a most successful man. But, as it turned out, the marriage did not take, just as old Henry Bell had predicted. Mr. Anders sailed for home alone, for Leticia refused to go with him. She was with child at the time, so it was considered perfectly understandable. I lost patience with her. She seemed to have become such a namby-pamby woman, with no starch to her at all. But there, she died when her daughter Celia was only a small child, so perhaps I am being unkind."

"I see. This is all very interesting, ma'am, but why did Miss Anders never have a Season?"

"She didn't want one," said Dolly Farrington, inventing wildly. "It is not generally known, but she is a bit of a bluestocking, and has even been heard to preach women's rights."

The duchess sank back in her chair, hand to her heart. "Never say so! And you invited her *here*? You know how Kendall loathes such females!"

The dowager shrugged. "Since she has moderated her views in recent years, I didn't see the harm of it. But harm has come to *her* at Castle Wentworth, and I am ashamed. I tell you, Eunice, I depend on you to help me right this wrong. After all, it was your aunt who started the gossip and your aunt who keeps feeding the flames of it. I consider it the least you can do."

The new duchess did not look at all happy about the situation, but she saw no way to refuse. Fidelity Grey's reputation was too well known to her. She sighed and nodded.

Before she could tax her mother-in-law with the impropriety of entertaining gentlemen, no matter how nearly related, in her bedroom, Dolly Farrington was gone. She had several other people to speak to. She was in a hurry.

Findle had had her instructions as well, and she spent a lot of time in the servants' hall, supposedly sewing but in reality passing on to all who came in the story of Miss Anders's wealthy American father. Charity Dawkins heard her and tried to dispute it, but no one listened to her. As Findle said, "How could a child like her know anything of the matter?" Ignored, all Charity could do was seethe.

Above stairs, Lady Cassandra was doing everything she could to help. Dolly Farrington, meanwhile, had gone to speak to Dudley Bell to make sure he knew the lies she was telling, and would aid in the deception.

At last she knocked on Celia's door. She found her in a welter of petticoats, shifts, and sandals, her trunks brought down from the box room, and her gowns spread over chairs and bed.

"I see I've arrived just in time, my dear," she said as she pushed a pile of lace-trimmed petticoats aside so she could sit down. "You know, you must not run away in this cowardly fashion. I never expected it of you."

"I told Viscount Drummond I didn't care if I was called a coward, and forgive me if I say the same to you, ma'am. I have learned of my background. I should not be a guest here."

"Of course, it is unfortunate your father was a footman. I can see why you are upset. But I knew about that when I invited you."

"However, there is no need for anyone else to discover the truth. You say they already know, thanks to our gossip? But right now they are hearing an entirely different version."

Celia sat awed through the telling, so stunned she could not even protest the lies.

"So you see, there is no need for you to go tearing off this way. In fact, if you do, all my work will have been for nothing. And it would make your uncle so unhappy, poor man, to say nothing of how *I* would feel! In fact, I will be most disappointed in you, Celia. And here I was, beginning to think you cared for me."

She eyed the girl shrewdly over the handkerchief she raised to dry eyes.

"My dear ma'am, no, no," Celia cried, coming to kneel before her. "You must not cry! It is just I feel such an impostor here. And this story you have invented does not change the truth of the matter a whit."

"No, of course not. But that is immaterial," the dowager said grandly. "The party lasts only two more days. Surely you can carry the deception off for that length of time. I assure you, when next you appear in company, no one will say or do anything that will make you uncomfortable. You have my word on that."

Celia rose and went to stare out the window. Could all this be true? Would it be all right to remain? She had hated the thought of leaving a moment before she had to, and she knew very well why. It was because even if there was no way she could ever marry Viscount Drummond, she wanted to be near him for as long as she could. Bless Dolly

190

Farrington, she thought as she turned back to her. She's given me a way to do just that.

Miss Anders did not come down for nuncheon, nor did she appear later, when some of the ladies set off for a sedate walk around the lake. But neither did a traveling carriage arrive at the front door to be loaded with baggage before Mr. Bell and his niece took a hurried departure.

The first time any of the guests saw Celia Anders again was just before dinner. She came into the drawing room wearing the pale green muslin gown that became her so well. This evening she had had the maid dress her chestnut hair high, and her carriage was regal. Viscount Drummond thought her superb.

On his return to the castle, he had heard all about the dowager's contrivances, and after giving a shout of laughter had hugged her so hard she had feared for her ribs.

Now he watched Dolly Farrington go quickly to Celia to put an arm around her and escort her into the room. He saw that everyone greeted her kindly, although some more warmly than others. Even the new duchess made a point of speaking to her for several minutes, but the duke kept his distance, watching her nervously. Not only Drummond, but Celia, wondered why.

Bart Whitaker took her in to dinner, and he was so easy and witty, Celia found herself laughing at his pleasantries. The ice inside her began to thaw. On her other side, his cousin, Earl Castleton, discussed the play with her.

She tried not to look at Drummond too often. He had not spoken to her before dinner, but perhaps that was because she had come down so late, and the dowager had been so much in evidence.

When the ladies left the gentlemen to their port later, Celia found she was bracing herself again. She had not liked the way Mrs. Grey had barely taken her eyes from her all through the long meal, almost as if she expected such an ill-bred miss to begin eating with her fingers. And then there had been the twins, trying so hard to appear nonchalant, yet darting horrified little glances at her whenever they thought she was not looking.

Responding to Lady Cassandra's welcoming smile, Celia went to sit beside her and endure a chat about the weather. Tonight, however, she was not bored, she was grateful. Since she had been at the castle, she had discovered women had a way of getting at you if they wanted, and with the men absent, now was the time they might well go on the attack.

Lady Flowers did try to introduce the subject of the gossip that had been going around about Celia, pretending to be appalled. Mrs. Grey was fervent in her agreement. To Celia's surprise, both were put firmly in their places by the new duchess.

"I do not see any reason why any of us, being ladies, should dignify these loathsome untruths by discussing them. That is merely to encourage the gossip who started them to continue. I tell you I will not have it at Castle Wentworth! My mama-in-law and I are in complete agreement on this head. Isn't that so, dear ma'am?"

A startled Dolly Farrington nodded, sending the duchess the warmest smile that lady had ever received from her.

When the gentlemen came in, Charles Danforth came to Celia's side at once, to whisper he had been so inspired by her courage and dignity, he intended to write an epic poem and dedicate it to her. Celia tried to look properly grateful.

It seemed an age before Viscount Drummond approached her. But after waiting for him to do so all evening, now Celia found she had nothing whatsoever to say to him. How perverse she was.

As she discovered, it did not matter, for the viscount had plenty to say to her.

"I think it is time we set a trap for Charity Dawkins, ma'am," he began. "My valet tells me she has been following me. Tomorrow, after our last rehearsal, I want you to meet me in the north gallery. No one ever goes there. We'll have it to ourselves."

Quickly, he handed her a note folded into a tiny square. "To make sure little Miss Dawkins will be there, I want you to leave this lying about your room when you leave it in the morning. Make sure it is somewhere obvious. I suspect the child has been in and out of all our rooms. Petson's mentioned he's found some of my things disarranged."

"But that's awful! Why, she might have read private letters, even journals," Celia said as she tucked the note away. She hoped no one had seen the exchange, but she dared not glance around.

"Probably that was what she was looking for. And I think she spent a lot of time eavesdropping, too. Dolly confessed she had told Lady Cassandra about your father one afternoon in the blue drawing room she frequents so often. It is entirely possible Charity Dawkins was in the room at the time, hidden from sight.

"We'll soon find out." He leaned closer, his eyes intent.

"Much as I regret it, Celia, this is not the time or the place to make love to you. But I look forward to doing so as soon as possible. I am going to marry you, you know. No, no arguments now! You don't want me to get testy, do you? Lose my temper?"

When Celia refused to answer him, he chuckled.

Seventeen

THE REHEARSAL NEXT morning was a disaster. Celia
wondered how Earl Castleton could look so cheerful
when right before his eyes the actors, one and all,
managed to forget their lines, bungle their entrances and exits, and stand about looking wooden.
The twins had even reverted to high-pitched giggles again.

When she mentioned this to him as everyone
began to disperse, he only grinned. He told her a
terrible dress rehearsal meant a flawless performance. He had never known it to fail.

Celia looked around. She'd noticed Charity
Dawkins had come late to rehearsal, and she wondered if that was because the little girl had been in
her room reading the viscount's note.

Now Celia saw that Charity was already gone,
and she wondered anew if she was even now making her way to the north gallery. As she aligned the
pages of her copy of the play and put it where she
would be sure to find it that evening, she could see
Viscount Drummond deep in conversation with
Bart Whitaker. When he hurried away, Celia wondered why Mr. Whitaker was smiling down at her,
almost as if he knew a delicious secret she did not.
Surely Drummond had not told him about the two
of them, had he?

She worried about this all the way to the gallery
tucked away on the third floor of the north wing. It

194

was not a pleasant place, even on the brightest day, for no sunlight ever entered its long, narrow windows. As she came in, Celia looked around nervously, wondering where Charity was hiding, if indeed she was even there. The room was almost bare, although there was a massive wooden chest against one wall, and of course there were all those floor-length heavy velvet draperies at the windows.

Drummond was waiting for her, idly inspecting a dark oil of one of the early Farringtons. He turned when he heard her step, holding out his hands to her and smiling. She found it impossible not to respond.

"Dearest, I can't tell you how glad I am you have come," he said loudly as he squeezed her cold hands. "You aren't nervous, are you? But no one will know of our meeting, love. I promise."

He bent closer then to kiss her cheek. Celia started as he put his arms around her. As his lips moved to her ear, he whispered, "Be careful! She's here."

Celia felt herself begin to tremble as his hands caressed her back and his mouth captured hers. She knew she could not pull away from him lest she give the game away, for his note had been very amorous. At the time, she had wondered if Charity might not smell a rat, for what woman would leave such a thing lying about for anyone to read?

But it was impossible to concentrate on that—or anything—when the viscount's kiss was making her feel all warm and tingly and abandoned. Her knees began to shake, and a very strange warmth spread over her body.

"Darling Celia," he said at last. Celia kept her eyes closed, although she was glad his voice had been more than a trifle unsteady. It would have been so unfair if he had been in perfect control of his senses when she was so bereft of hers.

"We must make some plans. I intend to speak to your uncle before we leave the castle, to ask his permission to pay my addresses."

Celia's eyes flew open.

He laughed down at her then, his eyes full of love and amusement. "Although it's a bit late to be doing that, don't you think. Mmm, as far as we've gone up to now, I mean? But I intend to marry you with as much pomp and ceremony as possible.

"Ah, but you're a witch, for see how you've cast your spell over me. But you know that, don't you, sweet?" he asked. Then he whispered, "Say something. Quickly!"

Celia had to clear her throat before she could obey him, and his wicked grin flashed again. "As to that, why, we will have to see, sir," she said, trying wildly to think of something innocuous to say. But would any woman talk of common things when she had just been kissed by a master at the game? Drummond had let her go, and now he was tiptoeing over to one of the windows. He made an impatient gesture, and Celia said, "I do hope my uncle will agree, dearest, for I am just as eager as you to . . . well, what I mean to say is . . ."

Drummond had reached the window, and he hesitated, as if to hear the end of her sentence. At last he reached out and pulled the drapery aside.

Even knowing she was there, Celia had to gasp when Charity Dawkins was revealed, pressed back against the window and staring at them both, her mouth agape.

Drummond took her by the arm. "And now, Miss Dawkins, we have you finely, do we not? You have been very busy about the castle these past few weeks, haven't you? No, don't bother to deny it. For how did you know I was going to meet Miss Anders here if you had not stolen into her room this morning to read the note I wrote to her?

"Come along. I'm taking you to the dowager and your mother. Your day here is over, you repellant little brat."

"William," Celia said, her voice a warning.

"Quite right. We'll let the dowager deal with her. She'll do it so much better," he said as he forced Charity to walk beside him. Celia fell in on her other side.

Looking down at the child's sullen face, she could see no remorse there. Instead, there was an almost calculating expression in her pale blue eyes. Somehow Celia was sure she was thinking frantically of a way she could escape this trouble unscathed.

When they reached the main hall, Drummond inquired for the dowager, and asked Bogle to have Mrs. Dawkins join them in the blue drawing room at once.

Dolly Farrington was big with questions, but Drummond refused to answer her. "Let us wait until the child's mother is here, ma'am," he said as he pushed Charity down in a straight chair and stood guard over her. "There isn't any sense repeating the thing over and over. It's not a pleasant subject."

"My dear ma'am, is there anything wrong?" Drusilla Dawkins asked as she hurried into the room. She had come from the luncheon table so quickly, she still grasped a napkin in her hand. "Why, Charity! What is it, dearest?"

"Sit down, Mrs. Dawkins," the viscount said. It was not a request, and looking at him apprehensively, she was quick to obey.

"Miss Anders and I have just discovered your daughter in the north gallery, ma'am," Drummond began.

Mrs. Dawkins smiled and settled back in her chair, more at ease now. "Yes, she often wanders about the castle, for she is so interested in everything here, the antiquity and history. But then, Charity has always been precocious. Why, I remember a time when—"

"She was not in the least interested in furthering her education, ma'am," Drummond interrupted. "Miss Anders left a note in her room this morning that I had written to her making the appointment. Your daughter had to have been there to read that note, for she was in the gallery before us, hidden behind one of the draperies."

"No," Mrs. Dawkins exclaimed, hand to her heart, "you shall not say such things about my darling little girl! I am sure it was just a coincidence. Perhaps she heard you coming, and frightened, slipped behind the draperies to hide. Of course, she could not reveal her presence when Miss Anders joined you. Yes, that is how it was, wasn't it, darling?" she implored, staring hard at Charity.

Before the child could agree, the viscount said, "I rather think not, ma'am, although I'll allow it's a clever solution. But today's debacle is not the only thing Miss Charity has done here."

He reached into his pocket and withdrew the tiny piece of twine he had found. "This is what she tied across the servants' stairs so a footman she disliked would fall down them. He told me he had been given orders to keep her out of the breakfast room."

"Good heavens," Dolly Farrington said. "Are you sure of that, William?"

"How dare you accuse my daughter of such a thing, sir?" Drusilla Dawkins demanded. "You have no proof! Besides, Charity is only a child—sweet, innocent."

"Believe me, you are the only one who sees her in such a light, ma'am. But you're quite correct. I can't *prove* Charity was the one who tripped the footman any more than I can *prove* she put poison in the butler's decanter and made him so ill."

"No, Bogle?" the dowager asked, but Drummond raised his hand and she fell silent.

"Neither can I *prove* she was the one who started the gossip that Harriet Hadley is a thief, or *prove* she's the same person who stole the dowager's ruby pendant and put it in Miss Hadley's sandal for a maid to find. Miss Anders foiled that scheme."

Celia glanced at Charity, who stared back, her expression so malevolent, Celia drew back instinctively. It was then she believed for the first time that Drummond had been right about the child all along. She *was* evil.

"But I'm sure of all the things I've mentioned, just as I'm sure she was here in this room the afternoon you spoke to your dear friend Lady Cassandra about Miss Anders's background, Your Grace. No one else in the castle knew anything about it. And, Mrs. Dawkins, can you honestly say, knowing her as well as you do, that you think the gentle Lady Cassandra depraved enough to start such gossip? Well, ma'am, can you?"

"Of course my aunt did not do it," Mrs. Dawkins said, her face white except for the two patches of red she wore on her cheekbones. "But that is not to say my dearest Charity did it, either!"

"Your dearest Charity is the most vicious, unprincipled, nasty little piece of work I have ever seen," the viscount told her. "No, keep your seat. If you do not, I'll summon some footmen to restrain you and your daughter, too. And I hardly think you would want any of this to go beyond this room, now, would you?"

He did not wait for an answer. Turning to the silent Charity, he said, "Where did you hide that day? Behind the draperies again? Or were you in the next room with your ear pressed to the door?"

He must have seen her eyes move, for he went to the wing chair pulled up to one side of the fireplace. "Ah, so this is where you hid, your legs tucked under you. Her Grace and Lady Cassandra could not have seen you here unless they walked the length of the room and looked, could they?"

"I have heard quite enough," Dolly Farrington said, rising to ring the bell and glaring at both the Dawkinses. "You will order your maid to start packing at once. In fact, I'll send some maids to help her, since I want you both off the castle grounds as soon as possible.

"Ah, Bogle, have a footman take this child to her room. He is to make sure she remains there. In fact, he'd better not let her out of his sight."

"But—but ma'am," Drusilla Dawkins pleaded as Charity was marched away. "You cannot believe the viscount! I do not know why he would do such a terrible, terrible thing, accusing my little girl. But you must see she could not have done the awful things he has laid at her door. Truly, she is the dearest child, and no trouble to anyone!"

"On the contrary, she will be a great deal of trouble to any number of the human race if you do not take her in hand, and at once. I only pray it is not too late," Drummond said. His voice was not scornful now, only serious. "I suggest you have a candid talk with Miss Charity, although I doubt she'll admit anything, even to you. She is not normal. You will have to have her carefully watched, and you must learn to discipline her. And never let her get anywhere near a loaded pistol or a knife. She is, I believe, quite capable of murder."

"I refuse to listen to such—such slander!" Drusilla Dawkins exclaimed. "And I would remind you, m'lord, there are laws against it. Take care you do not find yourself in court!"

"I doubt that very much, ma'am. In fact, I think when you have had some time of quiet reflection, you will recall many instances that point to your daughter's direct intervention. But you must stop excusing her, and stop refusing to see what is right under your nose. If you do not, only heartbreak lies ahead."

Drusilla Dawkins glared at him for a moment before she whirled and ran from the room. Only her little sobs broke the silence as she hurried away.

Dolly Farrington lay back in her chair, looking white and exhausted as the door slammed. Celia knelt beside her to chafe her hands.

"Is it true, William?" Dolly asked weakly. "Did that horrid child really do all those things?"

"Yes, I'm sure of it," Drummond said as he poured three glasses of sherry. "Of course, we had no proof until this morning."

"It was clever of you to trick her that way," Her Grace said as she took the glass he offered. "But when I think of it! My dear old Bogle might have died, and Fred Givens! To think he had to suffer such pain merely because he relayed an order. And Miss Hadley, Lady Powers—even Celia here—all her victims.

"I have to wonder, though, what Charity had in mind for me."

"We'll never know, since she didn't get the chance to carry it out," Drummond told her, smiling now.

"It was probably poison, too," Dolly Farrington told them. "I don't use the back stairs, and Bogle and his minions keep a careful eye on me now that they consider me decrepit."

"Drink your sherry and stop fishing for compliments, ma'am," her godson ordered. "You decrepit? What a whisker!"

Kendall Farrington saw Mrs. Dawkins and her daughter leave Castle Wentworth an hour later. He had just returned from a ride around the estate, and was about to mount the steps as a groom led his hack away, when he saw a cavalcade coming down them. He wondered at the number of footmen for such a small amount of baggage, and the presence of a stern-faced Viscount Drummond on guard at the door.

Although the duke would be the first to admit he was in no way needlewitted, he realized from the indignant expression Mrs. Dawkins wore that some unpleasantness had to have occurred.

Not wanting to be involved in any way, he merely tipped his hat to the woman and her glum-faced child and wished them a pleasant journey as he passed them before he scurried by Drummond into the sanctuary of his castle.

Eighteen

As soon as the carriage containing the Dawkins family and their maid had disappeared around a bend in the drive, William Welburn went searching for Celia. Somehow she had disappeared soon after the three of them had finished their sherry in the dowager's favorite retreat only an hour before.

He did not find her in any of the other ground-floor salons, nor in the library, where an inquisitive Duke Ainsworth demanded the reason for the Dawkinses' sudden departure. Drummond promised a most detailed telling another time before he hurried away.

Eventually he had to go to her room, where a startled maid told him miss had gone out for a walk.

The viscount hoped he would find her shortly. It was midafternoon now, and the time was fast approaching when he would have to get ready for the play. The guests and cast were to have a lavish tea at five, for the play would begin at eight. At its conclusion, the dowager's champagne supper would be held. All during that time he and Celia would be surrounded by people. Tomorrow they would be leaving the castle.

Oh, it was not that he could not pursue her in London. It was just that he did not think he could bear to wait that long. He had said he would marry her. Indeed, he had said it a number of times. But

Celia had never agreed. In fact, on that day in the garden he had told her of the gossip about her she had told him there could never be anything between them.

There was little chance she had changed her mind. The fact that the dowager had stifled the gossip could not erase the truth. Her father was an illiterate footman. He knew that would weigh heavily with her. Somehow he must convince her it did not matter, that nothing mattered but their love.

How he was to do that, when he could not even find her, he did not know. He could not see her anywhere around the lake, or in the still-dormant gardens.

Suddenly he remembered the little shelter deep in the woods where they had met before, and his step quickened. When he reached it, she was there, sitting on the crude bench, staring off into the woods. She sat so quietly, it was like looking at a statue. Afraid he would startle her, he called her name softly.

Celia turned and watched his approach, her face pale and composed. She had spent an hour there, remembering all the times they had been together—his words, his smiles, his embraces. Especially his embraces, and those wonderful kisses. She knew she would remember everything all through the lonely years that lay ahead.

"Somehow I knew you would find me here, m'lord," she said as he joined her on the bench. As he started to draw her into his arms, she put both hands on his chest.

"No, please don't," she said. "It will only make it harder."

Drummond sat back, balancing his shoulders against the rough wood. His top hat tipped over his eyes. "So, you've made your decision, have you,

Celia?" he asked, his voice as calm and courteous as hers. "I am sure it is a most reasoned, honorable decision, too. You are going to give me up—ah, I bow in homage to such *nobleness!*"

"It is nothing to make fun of, sir," she cried. "How can you mock me?"

"Because, although as a gentleman I must object to your spending a miserable life, I find I object to *my* doing so much more strenuously. Especially since there is no need for it.

"I love you. And you love me. No, there's no sense denying it. I have felt your love every time I've held you in my arms. I've seen it in your glorious hazel eyes, heard it in your sweet voice. It's useless to pretend otherwise."

Celia bowed her head and stared down at her clasped hands. He was right, of course. She did love him. Too much to marry him, she told herself, and felt stronger immediately.

"What I feel or do not feel about you does not alter the situation, William," she said in the little silence that had fallen between them. "Perhaps it's just as well I'm not given to romance, and never have been. Indeed, I've always found such things in novels and the theater amusing. Yet here in real life we have you, fourth Viscount Drummond, courting Celia Anders, a footman's daughter. It would make a wonderful farce, wouldn't it?"

"Now, you mock me for being noble, trying to protect you. Have you ever considered I might be doing this for myself?"

"What nonsense is this?" he demanded roughly.

"I do not think I would have a happy life as your wife, sir. The haut ton is slow to forget, and would be quick to remind me of my unworthiness every time I braved their ranks. I would prefer to marry a commoner than suffer their scorn day in and day out."

"There will be nothing of the kind, and you know it! You saw how easily the dowager turned the tables on everyone in the castle. If such things bother you, we will just perpetuate the myth of a wealthy, absent American father. But let me assure you, I don't care if the world knows your background.

"Now, when are you going to stop arguing with me? I want to make love to you, not talk. Talk makes me testy."

As he spoke he pulled her close. To his amazement, Celia began to struggle, and he let her go. As soon as she was free, she rose and backed away from him.

"You don't believe me! Why don't you take me at my word? Why do you think what I say is unimportant? *You* don't want to talk! *You* want to make love! What *I* want doesn't matter. Well, I've told you how I feel, and I repeat it now. I will not marry you, and I'd appreciate it if you would leave me alone!"

She felt the tears welling up inside, and afraid she would betray herself, she turned and ran.

William Welburn watched her flee, her navy cloak streaming out behind her. He hoped she would look where she was going, if she could see through her tears, that is. Then his jaw set hard. He wished he could have convinced her this afternoon, but if it were not to be, he still had another way. Best he get on with it, he told himself as he followed Celia down the path.

By early evening Castle Wentworth hummed with activity. Maids and footmen ran about, bringing freshly pressed gowns and elaborate costumes, pausing only to whisper of the evening to come.

Nervous laughter could be heard in the hallways whenever a door was opened. The lavish tea had been consumed and cleared away, and in the basement kitchens finishing touches were being put on the fancy supper that was to follow the performance. Mrs. Pope, the housekeeper, dealt with a number of problems with massive calm, and one more time Bogle counted the bottles of champagne he had icing. Even Eunice Farrington was caught up in the excitement of a castle *en fête,* for she decided to wear one of her new Paris gowns.

By seven-thirty, carriages from miles around were arriving, their gaily dressed occupants all agog to see the visitors from London. By eight, everyone was seated in the largest drawing room and the footmen stationed on the sides of the room were extinguishing the candles burning in sconces there. When only those before the makeshift stage glowed, two maids dressed in matching white gowns pulled the curtains aside.

Celia had slipped into her place close to the stage only a short time before the hour. She was glad the dimming lights hid what she was sure were traces of tears.

The audience was given a minute or so to admire the first set, a reproduction of a library, before Harriet Hadley swept in, exclaiming over her shoulder, "Never say so, dear Father! Why, I am sure you are wrong! The Quentins have always been such wonderful neighbors!"

"I'm not wrong! I'm never wrong, you silly chit," Mr. Grey roared as he marched in behind her to take a seat at the desk. The audience laughed, and the play Dolly Farrington had chosen was in full swing at last.

The first act passed quickly. Celia had to prompt a twin only once. And she could sense the audience was enjoying itself, laughing, exclaiming, and clapping in all the right places. By the time the curtain closed, she knew the play would be a tremendous success.

Viscount Drummond had a lot to do with that. As the villain of the piece he was superb—menacing, dark—with a silky manner that had a young lady seated directly behind Celia gasping. Once someone even hissed.

If only he had not looked so impossibly handsome and dear in the full-skirted whaleboned coat, knee breeches, and powdered wig of the last century. Celia wondered he had not looked her way even once, and she felt a little heartsick until she reminded herself she was being ridiculous. Hadn't she told him she would have nothing to do with him? How could she resent it when he took her at her word at last?

She looked out past the audience, all talking of the play with great animation, to where Charity Dawkins had so often sat watching rehearsals. She wondered what would become of the child and her mother. She'd heard Lady Cassandra had been so devastated to learn it was her great-niece who had been the cause of all the trouble, she had retired to her room in floods of tears.

Looking around now, Celia saw she had not made an appearance this evening. The dowager stopped beside her chair to chat for a moment, and she voiced her concern.

"Dear Cassie is such an innocent!" Dolly Farrington said, shaking her head. "She is taking this personally, you know. But tomorrow I'll point out Drusilla Dawkins is her niece only by marriage, and that horrid little Charity obviously takes after her mother's side of the family. There is nothing to worry about!

"I must take my seat again. I see the footmen are extinguishing the lights for the next act. Isn't this the greatest fun? And isn't Drummond marvelous? But I don't have to tell you that, do I, my dear?" she added with an arch smile.

Celia forced herself to smile back, although she had seldom felt less like doing so. Indeed, she had a nasty little headache throbbing at her temples already. Would this evening ever end?

It was early in the last act when the play began to go awry. At the time, the hero and heroine had just left Bart Whitaker alone in the library, and David Powers had ushered Viscount Drummond into the room. Celia was thinking what an excellent butler he made, when Drummond said something she had never heard in the script before.

"You here, Bruce?" he asked Mr. Whitaker. "But of course you are, since you're Fenton's best friend. When he marries, you'll be a lonesome man."

"No doubt you're right," Whitaker replied with such aplomb Celia was stunned. But she had to wonder what had come over Drummond. He had never had to be reprimanded for improvising as Charles Danforth had.

"I loved someone once," the viscount said now, and Celia stiffened. "I loved her to distraction."

"What happened?" Bart Whitaker asked, sitting down on a corner of the desk and picking up the pipe he had discarded earlier.

"She wouldn't have me. I guess she didn't think I was worth the trouble. It was very sad to discover that although my love was so strong that nothing else in the world mattered, she did not feel that way. Oh, there was a small problem—nothing that couldn't be overcome in time, but she did not care to take the risk."

"I'm sorry to hear it, old fellow. Perhaps if you tried again?"

Celia sat frozen in her seat, her eyes never leaving the stage. She felt she was suffocating, until she remembered to take a shallow breath.

Suddenly, William Welburn walked over to her, and she shrank back in her seat. He looked down at her directly as he said, "If I thought it would help, I'd do so immediately. But without some encouragement, I hesitate to put my love to the test again. Refusals are so painful."

He paused, his dark eyes burning down into Celia's. Behind her, she could feel the audience stirring, and a low hum of whispered conjecture begin. She knew Drummond was waiting for her to give him that encouragement, but she could not move.

At last he held up his hands as if in defeat, and, turning back to Bart Whitaker, slipped easily into the villain's role again.

It was just as well no one needed any prompting, for Celia ceased listening to the play from that time on. Not even when the twins were murdered, the villain discovered, and the hero and heroine united at last did she show any sign of life. Only when the audience began to clap and cheer as the play ended did she slip from her seat and leave the room.

Behind her, a bemused Dolly Farrington watched her go, her eyes sad. So Miss Anders had denied William, had she? And he, who had never truly loved before, was taking the matter so hard, he had even dared to declare himself before a group of strangers.

She must do something! She could not bear to see him suffer! And surely Celia Anders must love him. How could she not, the dowager asked herself, even as she accepted the thanks and congratulations of the guests who crowded around to tell her how much they had enjoyed the play.

As soon as she could, the dowager went away. It would be a while before the players could remove their costumes and makeup. She would have time if she hurried.

She had expected to find Celia in tears in her room, but there was no trace of them on the girl's white face when she admitted her. Celia was quick to claim a terrible headache, and she begged to be excused from the rest of the evening's festivities.

"Pooh," the dowager told her as she took the most comfortable chair. "I know very well you only wish to avoid Drummond.

"What is wrong, Celia? Can it be you do not love him? I find that impossible to accept, even though I know I'm hardly impartial where my godson is concerned."

"Whether I do or not, I won't marry him, Your Grace," Celia said stubbornly.

"Then he will never marry, and what a shame that would be! Any man who would declare himself before such an audience as he had tonight is in love for life. How very dear you must be to him, and to think I never suspected it!"

Celia had turned a little aside, and all the dowager could see was her profile. But she could also see the way her lower lip quivered, and the way she was clasping her hands so tightly together, the knuckles were white, and she smiled to herself.

"Is it because of your father, Celia? You know, once I would have said a marriage between you two was not to be thought of, but William convinced me otherwise. Now I think it would be a marvelous match."

Still Celia said nothing, and Dolly rose.

"I beg you will relent, my dear," she said as she

went to the door. "But I will not tease you with it anymore."

It was very late before the last carriage rumbled away from the castle, and Viscount Drummond was able to seek his room at last. He had seen Celia was not among the guests when he came in with the other players to another round of applause, and he had steeled himself to endure an endless time. For there was no way he could absent himself from the festivities without hurting his godmother.

Only the twins had asked him why he had said what he had, and he had given them a careless answer. Others, he feared, knew only too well. Indeed, he had surprised a sympathetic look on David Powers's face, and Bart Whitaker's handshake had spoken volumes.

But he didn't want sympathy. He wanted Celia. He remembered that as he had stared down at her from the stage, he had seen nothing on her face but confusion. And possibly some horror, he told himself, his mouth twisting in a grimace. Well, why wouldn't she look horrified when he was embarrassing her so.

He went to the brandy decanter he had asked Petson to bring him and poured himself another snifter. There was little chance he would sleep. He had too much on his mind, so much, he had not heard Petson's disapproving sniff when he had dismissed him for the night.

Now he wandered over to the fireplace and settled down in the large chair beside it, to brood into the flames.

Later, he told himself it had to have been the slight draft he felt on his neck that made him turn, for there hadn't been a whisper of sound.

His hand was shaking as he put the snifter down on a table beside him, for there, standing in the doorway, was Celia Anders. He blinked, even rubbed a hand over his eyes as if to make sure she was not an apparition he had conjured up because he wanted to see her so badly.

As he watched, she came in and closed the door carefully behind her. To his eyes, she looked determined, determined and a little apprehensive.

"Can it be you have lost your way again, Celia?" he made himself ask courteously.

"No. I did lose it earlier, but now I've found it," she told him, never taking her eyes from his face. "Never mind that. I have something to say to you. The dowager duchess came to see me right after the play. She asked me why I wouldn't marry you. I didn't tell her."

She paused to take a deep breath, and he prompted her. "Can you tell me?"

She stared at him, her eyes troubled. "I am still not sure. I love you, but I know our marriage would not be easy. And I still don't think it is fair to burden you with my past, when . . ."

She was allowed to say no more, for Drummond swept her into his arms and kissed her as if he never intended to stop. Celia put her arms around his neck and surrendered completely.

At last he carried her over to the big chair and sat down with her on his lap. "I've never heard such silliness," he said. "And I was so sure you were a sensible woman. Burden, indeed! Besides, I'm not the least bit interested in your past. It's your future I'm concerned about."

He hugged her close for a moment before he took her face between his hands, his own face serious. "You were wrong, you know, sweet. What you want does matter to me. Strange, that. I've been all too arrogant with others in the past, but not where you are concerned."

213

He kissed her quickly before he added, "But what made you brave my room tonight? Not that I'm not delighted that you did."

"I couldn't wait till morning," she admitted, blushing a little. "Besides, I have been here before, sir, although in a less romantic way."

"But I thought you told me you weren't a bit romantic. Yes, I'm sure you said something like that."

Not allowing her the chance to answer, he bent his head and kissed her long and thoroughly.

"You don't kiss me as if you didn't care for romance," he remarked. "Can it be that you are a liar, Miss Anders?"

"No, I'm not a liar," she told him as he bent his head so his lips could explore every inch of skin from her ear to the low neckline of her gown. Celia's hands tightened on his shoulders.

"I just didn't *know*," she replied, a little breathlessly. "I've been so mistaken. And in the case of you and romance, my dear, I was *very* mistaken indeed."

Drummond smiled at her. "Not to worry, love," he said. "Everyone makes mistakes."

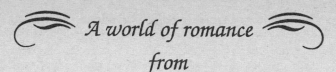

A world of romance
from
Barbara Hazard

Available in bookstores everywhere.
Published by Fawcett Books.